CHEER THE SICK

Black Shuck Books
www.blackshuckbooks.co.uk

First published in Great Britain in 2024 by
Black Shuck Books
Kent, UK

Versions of the following stories have previously appeared in print:
'Florabelle' in *The Ghastling #10* (2019)
'Cremating Imelda' in *Animal Literary Magazine* (2014)
'The Cherry Cactus of Corsica' in *The Shadow Booth vol. 3* (2019)
'The Fireman' in *The Ghastling #14* (2021)
'The Frost of Heaven' in *Winter Tales* (Fox Spirit Books, 2016)
'The Forlorn Hope' in *Out of the Darkness* (Unsung Stories, 2021)
'Grim' in *205 Word Stories* (Bag of Bones Press, 2022)
'A Little Star' in *Far Horizons #31* (2018)
'Veterans' in *BFS Horizons #15* (2023)
'Something Borrowed' in *Lore & Disorder* (2021)
'The Subtle Feast' in *Great British Horror 8: Something Peculiar*
  (Black Shuck Books, 2023)

Set in Caslon
Cover & interior design © WHITEspace, 2024
www.white-space.uk

978-1-917173-02-5

Cheer the
Sick

by

Verity Holloway

BLACK
SHUCK
BOOKS

For Gabriel, here from the start.

Contents

|The Luxury|

It is only a small quake this time, so I pay no mind to the lamp swinging above my head and continue my work. Between my household duties, I make labels for Uncle's bottles. He argues the handmade approach makes counterfeiting easier for our enemies, whoever they are, but our patrons adore my artistic touches: quaint, bespoke, more like a limited batch of miraculous perfume than a medicine.

Uncle's mansion sits at the centre of a sweeping country estate with mirrored dining rooms and guest quarters never used, but lavishly appointed. It's a far cry from the ramshackle cottage he first brought me to after my parents' deaths, so small I cannot now recall their faces, or what they thought of Uncle's enterprise, the penny bottles of Cheer-The-Sick he hawked from a barrow on the side of the highway, pelted by spray from passing carriages.

How far we have come.

Cheer-The-Sick is in demand like never before. The Duke of Monmouth partakes before battle and says it utterly numbs him to the fear of death. To enemies of the Empire he appears like a mad god of war, unstoppable, radiant. High society youths snort our product like snuff before approaching the daughters of visiting dignitaries. Confidence is an attractive quality. As for the girls themselves, they find a sprinkling on a fan turns them into sparkling conversationalists, the bright centres of the literary salons. Three years ago, the King was building a summer palace, and his daughters gaily suggested a bottle of our product be mixed in with the cement. Wouldn't you know it, the new royal abode is the envy of the crowned princes of the world. For hunting, the summer palace is unrivalled – deer wander up to the walls and extend their pink tongues to taste the mortar.

Cheer-The-Sick began as nothing but turnip-meal and soap shavings. And it would have stayed that way, were it not for Uncle's discovery: our deliverance, The Luxury.

The quake passes and I turn in my chair. The Luxury trots obediently along the line afforded by his leash, which Uncle has attached to the ceiling on a steel runner. The Luxury can walk the length of the room, clamber into his nest, and even use the chamber pot the way we trained him. Sometimes he canters, or, rarely, runs a length or two. Uncle tells me they enjoy plenty of exercise in the wild, though I know this is pure conjecture on his part. While we know nothing certain about The Luxury's genus or species, he is undoubtedly a mammal, and Uncle's books have taught me a great deal about bone and sinew and vascular intricacies. Whatever he truly is, it's important to allow The Luxury's muscles to do as nature craves.

"Water?" I put my hand to my mouth with the usual motion. The Luxury pauses, swivels his head towards me. A sylvian look, brown-eyed, silent. His water dish is full; he wants for nothing. Sometimes I like to ask him these things just for the novelty of conversing with someone other than Uncle.

There is another reason for fussing over him. Yesterday, in my work apron and stout boots, I assisted Uncle in the monthly harvest. Our patrons ask us why we haven't shipped Cheer-The-Sick around the globe, why we haven't purchased a small country with our earnings. For one thing, The Luxury himself is only so large. Uncle says he is fully grown, and I'm glad to hear it. Any larger and we would have trouble restraining him. More to the point, the horns grow in cycles totalling twenty-eight days. Harvest too early, and the shavings come away soft, spongy. The stumps bleed, though Uncle says the process doesn't hurt him.

Ground down and restless, he looks almost like a man.

Over supper, I put a suggestion to Uncle: "We could exhibit him."

"Someone would steal him."

"Not if we hired guards. The king would lay on security. He'd love to show him off at one of his parties."

"If we did it once, we'd never be free of invitations. People would come snooping."

I might enjoy being snooped on. As it is, my little workroom – The Luxury's enclosure – is windowless. In the long summer months, the earthy reek of him both repulses and intrigues me as I hunch over my desk and prettify another hundred labels with my quill. Sometimes, when I lie in my bed, I catch the lingering tang of him in my hair – fungi and leaf mulch and the healthy, equine salt of sweat – and feel, peculiarly, less alone.

Uncle dabs his dry lips with a serviette.

"No," he says finally. "The Luxury remains our secret."

It's a pity. The Luxury is pleasant to look at. He always has been, from the day Uncle brought him in from the snowy woods bundled up in his overcoat. He thought someone had abandoned their baby. We both did, rushing about the draughty cottage to find blankets soft enough for swaddling. When I held him in my arms – I was very young then myself, snaggle-toothed and bashful – the infant responded to my gestures and expressions as any other baby would. If it weren't for the wiry covering of brown hair, he would make any mother proud. As for the hooves, you could conceal those with a blanket.

He has grown to maturity in roughly the same time it would take a human to. We can safely surmise he is around twenty years of age, and he shows no sign of decline. His ears are placed where a man's would be, but they are long and velvet-smooth, not unlike a hound's, and just as mobile. His muscles are well-defined, but his sedentary condition has resulted in a little paunch. His nose twitches constantly. Perfumes bother him, as does smoke from the fire, and when the wind howls on a winter night, he turns his face to the ceiling and sighs. I am undecided as to what that might indicate.

But Uncle is right, his rarity will only tempt thieves. We believe he may be the last of a species hunted to extinction or wiped out by disease. Certainly none of Uncle's scientific literature offers an explanation. I pore over these books when Uncle retires to bed, studying the evolution of the canine skull from wolf to snuffling pug. Length of bone separates the hand from the paw, the predator from the prey. Uncle doesn't like me ransacking his library, but I feel strongly that my scientific curiosity makes me a better caretaker of The Luxury. Who knows what human pathogen, harmless to myself and Uncle, could take him from us? We must keep him – and ourselves – isolated.

And so it has been for as long as I can remember. I am a decent enough housekeeper. The work does not stimulate me, but I take a certain pride in relieving Uncle of domestic chores, freeing him up for his experiments. I can make a good suet pudding, and my arms are strong from cranking the washing mangle. Uncle comments on them more than I would like.

"Roll down your sleeves," he said on one particularly humid August day. "A woman shouldn't resemble an ironmonger."

He has never been shy about listing my physical defects, but, having little to compare myself to but pictures in books – which I understand to be much idealised – I am rarely hurt by his comments. The only time I was struck by one of his offhand judgements, I was thirteen years of age. The servants, of which we kept a modest handful until I was old enough to take on their duties myself, were celebrating All Soul's Night, using a mirror and a candle to tell which girls would find husbands in the coming year.

"Miss Katrin," called the chargirl, with whom I was always cordial, "come take a turn!"

But Uncle overheard, and forbade me. "Katrin will not be taking a husband. She must learn to run a house."

I was unaware of this. No husband? Girls seek husbands, that is what they do, according to every book in Uncle's library. What made me different?

That night as I performed my ablutions, I took stock of myself. I wasn't so hideous. My limbs were strong, my figure sturdy. My hair, on my head, my arms, my legs and sex, was abundant and pleasingly soft. I was noticeably taller than other girls my age, and my handspan wider than Uncle's, but I saw no logical reason why these things should preclude me from finding a match. Men, after all, came in a variety of designs.

I paid it no mind. I had my work to occupy me.

Once a year, around Easter, Uncle and I are summoned to the royal court to present our freshest bottles of Cheer-The-Sick and renew our royal patronage before noble witnesses. I put on my best dress and bonnet, and Uncle his finest suit, and we leave The Luxury in his enclosure with a pile of food and his litter tray. The trip is not a long one, and we never stay overnight, but still I like to explain to The Luxury where we are going, and how we would never abandon him. He trots over to me, hooves clicking on the tiles, and only turns away when I finish speaking. I like to think he almost understands.

Easter is fast approaching, and having been harvested recently, The Luxury is looking sorry for himself. I head to his enclosure with a treat of strawberry ice cream and my usual reassurances while Uncle beavers away in the lab, boiling and distilling and producing strange smells. In amongst The Luxury's chestnut curls, the twin stumps confront me. They will grow back. They always grow back. I admonish myself for encouraging this hangdog nonsense by bringing him sweetmeats. I leave the bowl on the floor just as an earthquake shudders up through the flagstones, startling us both. The ceiling lamp swings, casting monstrous, dancing shadows, and The Luxury sinks back to his nest of blankets, making himself small, covering his spoiled head.

"Peace," I tell him softly. "It will pass."

When the last of the aftershocks shiver away to nothing, I leave him lapping at the ice cream.

That night, Uncle calls for me. When I arrive at his chambers, he is swaddled in bed, his nightcap pulled down over his ears, red of nose and rheumy about the eyes.

"Supper tonight: plenty of garlic and spices. I must be well for our journey."

I keep my thoughts to myself. Garlic will only do so much for a bad cold. Despite the wondrous curative properties of our product, Uncle and I never partake of Cheer-The-Sick, not even under the direst circumstances. Uncle suspects addictive qualities, long-term side effects we may, as yet, be unaware of. Many a dealer of marvellous substances has undone himself sampling his own stash.

Uncle nonetheless registers my dubious expression as he sneezes into a sodden handkerchief. "I can't put the king off, Katrin."

"I could go."

"You?" He frowns, checking his nasal secretions for colour and consistency. "My dear, you'd be robbed. We'd be left with nothing."

"I've been with you dozens of times. You know I can drive the carriage. And I could take a guard if you care that much."

"A guard would rob you himself. Defile you. Leave you for dead and blame brigands."

I am of age. I whip up a bowl of garlic broth and go anyway.

The ladies of the court have a distinctive look – a uniform, to my eye – and I stand out among them like a pigeon in a cage of lovebirds. Their long hair hangs loose around their corseted waists, identically wavy in texture, epicurean brown brightening to the dark gold of buried treasure. Their skin is lightly tanned (I suspect by some artistry of powder) and they have all managed to nurture the same dainty figure, curvaceous without being matronly, their smooth flesh temptingly presented in low-cut gowns with wide, sweeping skirts. The court is noisy, always in motion, and I loiter shyly in a corner, feet together and hands clasped in front of me. I tell myself that if a handsome man were to walk in – I bring him to mind; lightly athletic, smiling, quick of wit with a book of botany in his coat pocket – he would be drawn to my unconventional drabness and fall in love with me instantly, and that all these buxom courtiers would silently despise me for daring to be plain, for having the courage they with their wealth and advantages could never comprehend.

Obviously, none of that will happen.

No one speaks to me, but there is much gossip as liveried servants glide about with trays of wine and canapes. A petite pair of noblewomen stroll by, and they notice me the way one notices a weed sprouting between paving stones.

"They have earthquakes daily out there," remarks one.

"Is it any wonder?"

The woman shoots a meaningful glance at my broad feet, and her companion titters behind her fan.

My moment arrives, and I am ushered by an attendant to the front of the gilded chamber where a scrolling throne waits upon a raised platform of claret carpet, plush as uterine lining. Lounging on the throne, the king is a smiling, athletic man of fifty-five, and his velvety manners put me at ease despite the whispering of the courtiers. I bob a quick curtsey and offer a sample of our latest batch, bottled up and completed with the label I fashioned by my own hand in the poor light of The Luxury's enclosure.

"A welcome sight, as always," the king says. He allows his dainty attendant to uncork the bottle and sprinkle a little onto a silver spoon. As always, I admire the whiteness of it, so unlike the shaven horns it derives from. The thought brings on an anomalous swelling sensation in my larynx, as if I need to cough or swallow, but I choose to ignore it, preferring to take satisfaction from the king's deep sigh of pleasure as he takes his first snort. "Rapturous! You have outdone yourself, my lady."

"I will gladly pass on your majesty's praise—" I begin, but further words dry up in my mouth. The king has extended the spoon to me, and his eyes lock with mine, pupils wide and black with bliss. It is not the prospect of stepping up onto the royal platform that daunts me. I do not partake of Cheer-The-Sick. I never have – indeed, Uncle has never thought to suggest such a thing – and my hesitation hovers on the cusp of rudeness.

Seeing my surprise, the king smiles at the mystified audience gathered around us. "How the simple country folk marvel at our degenerate ways. Please, my lady," he all but purrs. "Have a little fun."

God forgive me, what choice do I have?

And he is so frightfully handsome when pleased.

The king rewards me with a trunk of fine new clothes for myself and the promise of the same for Uncle when he is well enough to have his measurements taken. Next time we come to court, the stout little tailor tells me later, his majesty wants us to appear as important as we are. The chamber orchestra strikes up a whirling polka and the courtiers partner up on the dancefloor. I watch them, heart racing, but not with the self-conscious anxiety I have so far carried like a mantle. With Cheer-The-Sick glittering through my blood, I want to spin on my heels, to fight, to read every book ever written and pen my own response. I want to pluck a man from the court and ride him like a show pony. But the shadows grow long, and it is time to take my leave. If my carriage is held up by brigands, I tell myself, I am more than capable of taking them.

I return to Uncle with the good news about our forthcoming gifts. I find him in the parlour, hunched in a chair beside the dying fire. The cold has made him clammy as a hibernating toad, and when I blunder cheerfully into the room, his look of reptilian rage stops my feet and my tongue.

He chains me to The Luxury's runner and leaves me there all night.

It is colder in the enclosure than I ever realised. The Luxury keeps his distance, eyeing me owlishly from his nest of blankets while I quietly sob. Ground tremors keep me awake past dawn, and when the last glimmers of Cheer-The-Sick leave my body I am left with nothing but the hungover reek of my own shame.

Uncle unlocks me when he wants his eggs and coffee. Words of regret are not forthcoming. He leaves me to struggle to my feet, and I wipe the creases from my best skirt, finding it torn by the flagstones. I feel another sob squeezing its way up my throat, and do my best to supress it.

"Peace," says a quiet voice from the enclosure's farthest corner.

I go very still. When I force myself to look over my shoulder, I see him, The Luxury, burrowed into his blankets with only his curly head and the fine fur of his shoulders protruding. I experience a pinprick of memory: of holding him down like a sheep for the shearing; the hot, ossuary smell of the horns as Uncle worked the saw. He was shaking, I recall. Or perhaps it was another quake, passing up through The Luxury's body and into my own.

"You can vocalise."

He blinks. I tell myself I am exhausted, my nerves taut and overstimulated. His nose comes snuffing out of the blankets, and I think I see his mouth working, and my pulse flutters at the base of my throat in anticipation, but—

"Katrin! Eggs."

I jolt, and The Luxury slips back into his nest. "Coming, Uncle."

The trunk of clothes arrives from the palace on a rainy Friday, and the footman wants a tip. I am rarely permitted to carry cash – Uncle has all our provisions delivered on account – and when I mumble my excuses, the driver mutters something under his breath and turns on his shiny heel.

Uncle is in his laboratory, so I indulge my excitement and open the trunk to inspect my new dress. It is vast and architectural, an exoskeleton of dove grey silk with petticoats tightly pleated like the gills of dapperling mushrooms. I realise I had been afraid until now that the king would bundle me up in some candy-striped nightmare, an attempt to turn me into one of his snide lady courtiers. Evidently, his majesty is a sensitive man. This is the dress of an impressive woman, a serious woman, a woman with thoughts.

I prepare luncheon in my regular clothes, but I bring it to the dining room dressed in my new finery, wide as a door and glorious to behold in all our many mirrors. At the head of the table, Uncle's eyes widen, but he says nothing.

I take my place at his right hand, allowing the torpid *tick* of the clock and the softness of the silk enrobing my body to lull me into a pleasant, contemplative calm. Presently, I dab my mouth with a napkin. "I wish to claim my inheritance and study."

I am serene in my resolve. The sullen rumble beneath my feet is nothing but the shifting of the earth's tectonic plates.

"I beg your pardon?" Uncle says at last.

"My inheritance. My parents' money. You've mentioned it. With a little money of my own I can hire a maid to do the cooking and the washing, and with my free time I can study and write."

Uncle's nostrils flare over his soup. "And what would you write about?"

I lick my lips. I cannot say The Luxury, nor make mention of his strange new ability. I compose a noncommittal face. "I thought perhaps botany. A guide to the distillation—"

Uncle's fist slams down with shocking force. The bowls and spoons clatter and my mouth shuts like a trap. The cutlery jingles long after his outburst has passed and I realise another earthquake is upon us. Uncle stares at me, wordless in his fury, while the earth grumbles on beneath us. A vase topples from the mantlepiece and shatters. A childish fear threatens to overtake me; that Uncle, his rheumy eyes brimming with authority, commands these tremors, and that one day he will bring the house down around us if I fail to please him. I believe he told me so, once, when we lived together in that draughty shack strewn with bottles and papers and black weevils that converged on my blankets at night.

"See to The Luxury," he says. "And take that absurd costume off."

Poor creature, shaking in the corner.

I go to him, hands open to show I mean no harm. The quake has passed, but he knows as well as I do that the aftershocks will come and go for hours yet, and the waiting can be just as unpleasant.

"Peace," I tell him, since that is our word now, and ease myself down beside him. I am back in my house dress, rumpled and darned. What does it matter if I dirty myself further?

Those nut-brown eyes seem to speak, even if his lips do not. Where would he be now, had Uncle not plucked him from the snow that night twenty years ago? What manner of creature was his mother? Had a human male coupled with a deer? Is such a marriage of species possible? I envision leather-bound tomes bearing my name, halls of learned men applauding me as I stand at a lectern in my dove-grey dress, having presented my thesis on the discovery of this marvellous creature, this man-buck, this real, live God-Of-The-Wood.

His curls are soft when I lay my hand on them, but to my disappointment he recoils. My fault, I realise, like a fool. The only time I touch his head is to harvest his horns. Uncle tried all sorts in the beginning: his hair, his fingernails, his hot red blood. Something had to be of use, he kept saying. Men ground up mummified bodies stolen from Egypt and used them in medicine to great effect; how was this any different?

Egyptian mummies do not whimper when touched.

I speak to him as one speaks to a worried dog, soothing little nothings to ease the tension in his body. "Did you ever have a name?" I ask at last. "What name would you choose, if you could have one?"

Uncle wouldn't like that. You cannot attribute human behaviour to an animal, he says, and I, like any good scientist, agree. But looking into The Luxury's face, it is sometimes difficult to resist. He raises one furry shoulder, as if considering my question. The little pointed beard works up and down as he opens and closes his mouth.

"Christopher?" I suggest. The first name that comes to me, meaningless, given without thought, yet—

The eyes flick up. They regard me. Take me in.

Christopher it is, then.

It is only now that I see Uncle regarding me from the doorway. Whatever his impressions, he keeps them to himself.

Though a human name is inappropriate for an animal, Uncle decides a pair of trousers is a necessity if I am to be tending to The Luxury – to Christopher. We try several pairs, battling him into them, and he either tears them off or urinates in them every time. In the end, Uncle acquires a kilt to which Christopher grudgingly submits. He waddles around experimentally in his enclosure, legs wide like a cavalier sore from the saddle.

The kilt is yet another thing for me to launder, but Uncle seems keen to keep me occupied with the household minutiae ever since my journey to the royal court. As spring and summer fade, he demands ever more complicated dinners. Buttons need reattaching on a daily basis. When I sneak down the corridor to the library for an hours' reading, I will often find mystery spillages in need of immediate mopping before I can ever reach the door. I go to bed each night tired and frustrated, and when I dream, I dream of dirty dishes.

When I once more raise the subject of collecting my inheritance and hiring a housekeeper, Uncle only laughs into the pages of the book he is reading.

"I cannot imagine many self-respecting housekeepers would take orders from such a sloppy great brute as you."

As I hurry to my bedroom, I imagine I hear the beginnings of an earthquake, but it is nothing of consequence. Only the blood rushing in my ears.

The dining room mirrors become a scourge. I wear blouses with high necks and sleeves down to the wrists, but I often spy Uncle pointedly eyeing the dark down on my cheeks as I reach over to ladle out his soup. I feel an irrational shame followed by a hot blast of righteous anger. He has wiry grey hairs protruding from his nostrils, and his ears are fleshy and too prominent on his small head, and his scholar's stoop is painful to look at, and—

"I am not hungry," I say. "I think I'll retire for the night."

"Tread lightly, Katrin. Those big boots of yours make my head ache."

I traipse up to my room, noting with increasing frustration the rubbish he has strewn around the place, purely to make me pick it up. I find my mind turning to those women at the royal court, so elegant and refined. What would they say if they saw me now? I'd wager a whole crate of Cheer-The-Sick that not one of them has ever had to wash her own dishes, let alone those of a cruel old man.

That isn't fair, I tell myself as I sink into my bed. Uncle took me in when no one but the workhouse would. Were it not for him I would be no better off than the illiterate washerwomen who gather at the docks at night, lifting their skirts for all but the scabbiest of sailors. Yes, I'd read those secret books of Uncle's. This sloppy great brute knows a little of the world and how it operates. Perhaps all he wants is for me to acknowledge how fortunate I am under his care; to demonstrate a little of the feminine gratitude they write about in the family periodicals.

Where does one learn such a thing? After so many years of being told I am a lumpish, bovine thing, good for nothing but drudgery, how am I expected to blossom into something decorative and soft? In chemistry, such a thing would require a catalyst. In botany, fertilisation, or a graft. I lie awake long into the night, pondering my problem. I find myself half-dreaming of the king, of the way his comely eyes twinkled as he handed me the spoonful of Cheer-The-Sick.

I recall the sting in my nostrils and the butterflies in my blood. I am not so dense that I believe a king would pay me attention without such a powerful product at my fingertips, but all the same – I have it. Those twittering bitches at the court, for all their charms, will never possess half my power. I may not know what Uncle gets up to behind his laboratory door, but I know the day will come when he is too decrepit to do it alone. And then freedom will be mine.

I pull my nightgown over my head and swap it for my stays and undergarments. The dove-grey dress is like dark water in the candlelight, and when I lace it tight my body becomes a storm cloud full to bursting.

Christopher's enclosure, windowless, accepts me. I can smell him, all moss and fur, and when my candle illuminates him in his nest, his chestnut eyes shine like mirrors. I shake inside like a child afraid. His horns are almost fully regrown, ridged and curled and – finally, I see it – dangerous. He could gore me, I realise. Some would say he has every right.

With his eyes on me, I venture closer, bunch the slippery fabric of my skirts and petticoats in my fist and raise them an inch. I have come shoeless, my hair loose and tangled around my shoulders.

Furtively, Christopher watches. I grow confident and raise the skirts a little more, feeling the cool air on my calves. I consider removing my stockings, but I am unsure of how to do it gracefully. Usually, I tug and tug, grunting a little where the wool pulls my hair. I don't imagine such a thing would look very decorous, but as my doubts attempt to take root I hear Christopher in his nest of blankets: a snuffling *wuff-wuff* like a stag exhaling in the fog. He is smelling me, I realise with amazement. Without further hesitation, I kick down my stockings with either foot, fast and ungainly as a boy. The tiles are cold, but I pay them no mind; the sound has all my attention, the *clank* of chains as Christopher stands, an inquiring look in those dark eyes framed by a forest of lashes. The canine ears flick and swivel as my breath hitches, and with it, my skirts. He can see the full coarseness of my thighs now, my unmarriageable self, thick and furred and undeniably alive, if not like a human woman, then perhaps something better.

Clip-clop. Christopher approaches. To my dismay he is wearing the kilt Uncle forced upon him, barring me from the full extent of his velvet body. His nose twitches, responding to me; I wish for a mad moment that I hadn't washed, hadn't muted this hitherto neglected hormonal signal of mine.

It takes all my resolve to reach out my hand and place it on the curving juncture between his hip and waist. The fur there is sparse, but the flesh warm, yielding, hinting at the bunch and slide of powerful muscles beneath. For once he doesn't pull back. I have no idea what comes next, no plan, no strategy. But his great sylvan eyes are pleading and before I know it I am fumbling with the fastenings on his kilt, that fatuous human bondage of modesty, and it slips to the floor and it is nothing I haven't seen before but—

Christopher is looking over my shoulder. His ears are pinned back.

"My dear," says Uncle mildly, in nightcap and slippers. "I thought you were a burglar. I could have shot you."

His smile is a white slash in his shadowed face.

The leaves outside are turning brown. From my bedroom window I can see through their thinning canopy to the road beyond where I took the carriage to the royal court at Easter. I wonder what Christopher would make of such a view.

Uncle has been good to me this past month. Though he tells me this year's Christmas ball at the palace is strictly for professional men and women of good breeding only, he placates me with new reading matter – instructional tales for young ladies, but it's better than nothing – and has started picking up after himself when the mood occasionally takes him. Deliveries come frequently to the house. Home improvements, he tells me, for should we not live in comfort with all our hard-earned wealth? He has even taken to complimenting my cooking, which, I must admit, pleases me. I take pride in my work.

Speaking of work, we harvested The Luxury a week ago. Christopher, I mean. He took it well; I suggested to Uncle that instead of holding him down with my weight as I once did, I simply talk him through the process and comfort him with caresses. He is receptive to them these days, and Uncle not so quick to reproach me for indulging in human communication with an animal. The kilt remains a fixture. It's funny; it does so make him seem like a man.

I feel as if the frustrations of earlier this year, chafing me as surely as physical chains, have faded to a manageable ache. Uncle is ageing, he cannot deny it. He struggles to carry great piles of books to his laboratory, and his teeth give him trouble. I know the day will come when he takes me down the unlit corridor to that stinking chamber where Cheer-The-Sick is made and all the secrets of that intoxicating powder will be made clear to me. It will be my turn to take the carriage to court, to curtsey and flirt, to think on formulas and profit margins and the future. Old men die, of course, and the thought brings me no joy. I have no family but him. And yet, this grief presents the possibility of another kind of freedom, to unclip Christopher from his runner, to take him out into the world where fellow men of science will be hungry for my observations, crowding around me like flowers competing for light.

The trees shudder with another quake and I broaden my stance like a sailor to steady myself. I have made bread this morning, washed Uncle's second suit and hung it out in the cold garden, given the mirrors in the dining room a good dust (I may not wish to study my reflection, but standards must be upheld), and am making a start on a mutton soup for lunch. The broth slops as the kitchen rattles. I sigh, and once again put down the book I had been hoping to read while it simmers.

I go out into the tiled reception and call up the stairs. "Uncle? Everything alright?"

My voice rings in the empty space. He gets so utterly absorbed in his books. I've witnessed him sitting plum-dumb oblivious to quakes before, only glancing up with annoyance at the loudest breakages.

I leave Uncle to his own devices and hurry down to Christopher's enclosure. When I push the great heavy door to peek inside, Christopher is crouched in his nest under the swinging shadows of the ceiling lamp. I see him in flashing tableau; his darting eyes uneasy, his horns ground away almost to nothing. His face shines with tears, and when he sees me he keens highly, like a wounded child.

"Whatever's the matter?" I go to him with hands outstretched, but before I can reach him I stop, confused by the sight that greets me. The floor is wet with soap suds. Christopher's skin is pink, towel-dried, artificially scented with something lemony and acerbic. His skin. I can see his skin. He has been shaven. All but the top of his head, his forearms and his legs where they protrude from his kilt. He looks, to my horror, like any other man. Not in the endearing, costumey way of before, but something altogether unwholesome.

I get down on my knees to meet his eyes, but he cringes away. "Did Uncle do this to you?" I demand. I try to keep the outrage from my voice, but Christopher is keenly sensitive, now more than ever, and like a fool I realise that this is not Christopher's usual nest of blankets but a real human bed, made for two, with overstuffed pillows and a coverlet embroidered with chains of daisies. As the earthquake subsides and the light above us slowly returns to stillness, I stare open-mouthed at the changes made to the enclosure. A pair of armchairs face each other either side of a bookshelf, as yet unstocked with reading matter. Paintings have been hung, the kinds of pastoral confections Uncle has no time for: rosy-cheeked milkmaids smiling at great oblong cows festooned with prize rosettes.

Christopher miserably hugs his knees. This is a domestic tableau, a doll's house set for a game of mummies-and-daddies. A creeping sensation walks on eight legs down my spine. A small armoire resides against the wall beside the bed, and when I cautiously open the door, I find my dove-grey dress hanging there, like a suicide.

I thunder up the staircase.

"How dare you? You call yourself a scientist. What experiment warrants dressing him like a mannequin in a shop window?"

Along the bannistered gallery I pace, thumping on doors. How indecorous I must look, red in the face, my sleeves rolled up the way he hates.

"You *shaved* him," I shout, though I find no trace of Uncle. "What possible reason could you have? You've frightened him, terribly. Uncle! Where are you?"

He'll be mired in a book somewhere. My God, home improvements? This is what he was doing. That revolting little parody of a homestead. If Uncle wants to make Christopher more comfortable, he should let him see sunlight, let him trot amongst the trees as surely he was made to.

"Ruining his natural form like that," I seethe along the corridor. "And going through my things. My own possessions, mine—"

I throw open the door to Uncle's chambers. The bed is made, the fireside chair empty. His absence only fuels my anger, and I bustle along to his lab, readying my harshest words.

When I get there, the smell of Cheer-The-Sick hits me, a sour steam disgorged from a warren of glass retorts and ampoules. It physically unsettles me to know it's part of Christopher boiling away in there – a new feeling, one I haven't the time to analyse. My uncle is nowhere to be seen, but his desks are strewn with the work of the day, page upon page of arachnid scribblings in ledgers as thick as my neck. Illustrations are tacked to the walls, cross sections of bone and tissue, of stags and stoats and hairy creatures rendered hideous by dissection. It is impossible to tell the human subjects from the other assorted mammalian flesh. As I am rarely needed in the lab, I can't resist poking about a little, marvelling at the wealth of equipment Uncle never bothered to mention. I finger a pair of shiny steel forceps. In a jar of formalin, a human foetus the size of a fist curls in on itself, faintly porcine in its snub-nosed pallor. It's a curious sideshow distraction, but Uncle has always been more of a chemist than a biologist, and I can't help but wonder if having such a thing in the house without scientific intent is inviting – well, bad luck.

I force myself to look away. None of Uncle's recent behaviour is making sense, and I find my mind turning to dark possibilities. Some geriatric softening of the brain, perhaps. The beginning of the end. For all my dreams of independence, I feel somehow unprepared, taken aback by this new worry dampening the rage of moments ago.

Where is he? I scan his papers. Some of the ink is still wet; the gleam catches my eye. He's been composing a hypothesis. I see calculations, calendars, great copied swathes of Benevento's treatise on animal husbandry, the one that got him ejected from the Royal Stud. I read about the scandal back when my household duties allowed me a moment to myself. On another page, Uncle has sketched a dissected uterus, its layers of spongelike muscle rendered with care. Cheer-The-Sick has long been utilised by the royal midwives to aid that final, difficult push, and I wonder if Uncle is preparing to break his long silence on the matter of The Luxury and the true mechanism of its miracles. I would support such a move.

But that fails to explain that state I found Christopher in.

That unshakable sense of unease drives me deeper into the densely scribbled pages. Uncle writes of gametes and haemoglobin, of pheromones and the psyche. I am confronted by diagrams of dissected roe deer, of prostitutes exhumed and displayed in theatres of learning. Hooves and hands united on the slab. *A mutation of keratin,* he writes. *An otherwise healthy woman of sixty-eight in the Eastern Pyrenees was found to possess a horn of sorts, protruding painlessly from her forehead. Such things are not unheard of in the human race. Might they be induced?*

I can smell my own sweat.

Uncle does not lack aptitude in the visual arts. When I see my portrait, I know myself right away. He has captured my proportions, my expression of serious preoccupation, even the downy dark hair on my cheeks and lip.

Subject K: A woman of broad pelvis, swarthy, with a tendency towards stout robustness.

Nowhere is my name mentioned. Only this Subject K, her suitability, her youth, her affinity with The Male.

My likeness is gravid with child.

Calculations dazzle me. The time estimated for the offspring to grow its first horns. The amount of product yielded per subject. The space required for production and harvest. These numbers crowd my brain and turn my stomach. I rush over cold and wicked statements in Uncle's familiar hand, the writing I know from birthday cards and those first arithmetic lessons in that damp shack of his, so solitary until I came along. He was always keen to educate me in those early days. What changed?

I hypothesise the seed will catch without incident.

The earth begins to shake anew. I feel it under my feet, but only truly notice when the lamps begin to swing, obscuring my view of the papers. The preserved foetus hangs immobile, held by invisible wire inside its formalin womb.

As the windows rattle in their frames, I stride from the room. My cheeks burn and my fingernails, short and practical as befits a stout and robust housekeeper, dig painfully into my palms. As I sweep down the corridor to the gallery, I worry feverishly that he's down there right now, in Christopher's enclosure, doing something cruel and unseemly in my absence as the earth groans beneath us. And groan it does: a deep, cavernous lament like an arrow-shot stag, and a fresh shudder sends me lurching into the bannister with a cry.

"Katrin!"

Below me on the stairs, Uncle's shining head bobs. He is on all fours, clinging to a carpet rod popped loose by the quake. Around him lie pieces of broken plate and a dry cheese sandwich.

"Stay there," I call down. "It's a big one."

"My knees. You've ruined them."

At first, I think I've misheard him. I am edging towards the top of the stairs where he sprawls, trying to find a way to offer my hand and keep myself upright at the same time. Around the house I hear the smashing of glass and the complaints of old floorboards. Many hours of brooms and dustpans lie ahead of me. I catch the grand newel post and cling to it. I am able to hold on with one hand and extend the other to Uncle. Providing the bannister can take my weight, I will not fall to my death.

He is attempting an abortive crawl to the next step when a fresh tremor strikes and he cries out, teeth bared in pain: "I've fallen. All because you burned the soup. The soup, girl, don't look so stupid. I smelled it – scorched mutton! And with you nowhere to be found, I was forced to make my own luncheon. I should never have been down there and now—"

"I burned the soup." I hear myself say it, devoid of expression.

"—ruined everything. Help me up. My knees. I need a physician. I have important work to do and had you been in your blasted place—"

He thrusts out his hand, demanding mine. I watch it, quavering and liver-spotted, the hand that grips the hacksaw every twenty-eight days when The Luxury is at its strongest, its darkest, its most potent and lusty. And the other hand, clawed against the carpet now, I see it grasping Christopher's gentle head, forcing him down as if he were nothing more than livestock. A sheep for shearing, for breeding, for blessed burnt mutton soup.

The hairs on my body prickle. I draw back, hunch down, chin to my chest. For once in my life my desire is mine to claim. I am a bull, a ram, a horned charging thing, and the lurch of the earth only adds to my strength as I pitch forward, thrusting Uncle away from me with all the righteous force of a buck dispatching his first rival. Bone and sinew and busy canals of oxygenated blood – I watch him tumble. When he finally hits the tiled floor, far below us in the entrance hall, he continues to convulse. I realise after a moment of gasping horror that it is only the earthquake. The appearance of life.

I open the wide front door and allow the late autumn chill to sweep inside. Christopher is with me. He shies from the watery daylight. When I unclipped him from his runner, his eyes stared out searchingly from his horribly shaven face. He only followed when I gently tugged the leash. Somehow, despite everything, it was a joy to watch his hooves daintily trotting over Uncle's broken *tchotchkes* where they littered the halls.

When he sees Uncle face-down on the tiles, he sniffs the air and huffs. He understands the mechanics, if not the narrative.

"It's only you and me now…"

I let the sentence drift, the *now* of it ringing with hitherto fantastical possibilities. An inheritance. A future. A dress hanging in an armoire.

I hold the leash a moment longer, then let it pool on the floor. I fold my empty hands behind my back and look at Christopher. He must understand he has a choice, or rather, than I am putting one to him. A brown leaf blows in at our feet and he steps back, *clip-clop*, in timid reflection. He can't remember where he came from, I realise. He can no more go back there than I, having never seen it, can. My lips twist. With superstitious anxiety, I turn so I cannot catch a glimpse of the corpse. What would Uncle do if he had one parting shot? Perhaps my hesitation is vindication enough for him.

The wind touches my skin even through my petticoats. Arrangements must be made, for Uncle if not for me. Christopher needs feeding. I, too, need sustenance, I realise, as a wave of light-headedness cruelly mimics an aftershock.

When a hand touches my arm, I draw breath.

"Peace," Christopher says softly.

|Florabelle|

Communication with the dead? You ask this of a doctor? Legal documents of course spring to mind – funeral wishes, bequeaths and the like. But these are the messages of the living. The dead, on the other hand…

I think I have a story for you.

In my undergraduate days, I saw plenty of the dead. During those years of study with scalpel and saw, I was witness to – and the victim of – many a boyish prank involving the recently deceased. A glimpse into the daily shocks of medical school, the sights and smells and unforgettable sensations would turn the stomach of a grown man. But the young are a different species, aren't they? They are pliant, resilient, and above all concerned with the whims and amusements of the self.

It was the Christmas of 1864. I was a very young man, hardly fit to wield a shaving razor, never mind a scalpel. My friends and I had finished term, and to mark the joyous occasion we had orchestrated a rather vulgar tableau in the dissecting room. Myself, a boy named Black, and a handful of other students arranged a pair of flayed cadavers and a wired teaching skeleton in the manner of a gang of friends engaged in a game of cards. We purloined an empty bottle of port, and set out a glass for each cadaver. Black, with that great rolling laugh of his, wedged a clay pipe between the skeleton's teeth.

"There we have it. The ghosts of Christmas past."

And so we left them there for others to find. Black and I had agreed to meet Featherstone at the chop house that night. A fellow student, Featherstone played a tremendous game of cards, but was known to turn maudlin on matters philosophical. As we walked together, I advised Black to keep our mischief between us.

Black enjoyed my timidity. "He'll hear of it anyhow. And what business does he have being squeamish? He won't last long in our profession with that attitude."

I had meant it might offend Featherstone's sense of taste rather than his tolerance for grisly sights, which was no better or worse than ours. But Black could be bullish when challenged, and I regretted bringing the matter up when he found Featherstone at our usual table and announced without delay:

"I say, Featherstone. What use do the dead have for dignity?"

"Are you asking my opinion?" he said. He had bought drinks for the whole party and was already shuffling the cards.

"I live for it," said Black.

"That you even have to ask…"

"Humour me," he went on. "A vagrant dies, all but worn to the bone. Never heard a kind word in his life, dined on flour and water, and yet in death—! Oh, the *respect* as we cut him up like mutton."

"No matter the calibre of the man…" Featherstone began.

"Do we cut up men of quality?"

"No," conceded Featherstone. "But if we did, we would treat them with the respect we would hope for ourselves in such a vulnerable position, wouldn't we?"

"Vulnerable! My dear fellow, they are dead."

"And who are we to say what that means?"

Black laughed. He turned to me. "Are you taking notes?"

"Well…" I ventured mildly. "Perhaps the soul, wherever it may reside, harbours affection for its former vessel?"

"So we should be careful with a ghost's discarded overcoat?"

"It's a moral question, Black. Metaphysical. The point is, we don't know, so we must surely err on the side of caution."

"You weren't especially cautious today, posing that charwoman up with cards and—"

Featherstone glared. I admit, I regretted my actions, as common as they are for a student of the medical arts. In my heart I agreed. No matter what ugliness we must partake in as we hone our craft, the sentiment of human dignity must prevail.

Black took a deep guzzle of ale. "My dear fellows, if the dead have feelings, so do stones. So does that plate. If dead men are calling to us from beyond that dark veil, telling us to mind what we're doing with their bones, well, they ought to shout louder."

Featherstone looked thoughtful. "I imagine when I die, my former vessel will mean little to me."

"Oh, don't tell me you're a Spiritualist!"

"No. But I imagine if I could communicate, anything I said would be concerning…" Here, he was embarrassed. "Well, love."

There we dropped the subject. Why spoil a perfectly pleasant Christmas evening, when we were all so weary from our studies, unwilling to return to our draughty lodgings? Featherstone cut the cards, and Black ordered more drinks. We passed the next hour or two engrossed in our game, and forgot our good-natured quarrel.

Now, remember, we were students, so had little of value to bet. But bet we did. Blame the ale, blame the merry season, but we played a competitive game and Black lost to the tune of ten shillings. More than a week's rent.

Black drained his drink. "You've cleared me out, gentlemen. I have nothing to offer you except… well, lemon drops!"

He took a paper bag from his coat and offered it to us. I took a sweet, but Featherstone would not.

"Don't look like that, old man," said Featherstone with his customary lenience. "We'll call it a night and settle another time."

Black bristled. "Charity, is it? I can pay. You sit there. No, you too, Gower. You sit there and wait. You'll get your ten bob."

This was the last we saw of Black. Oh, we saw his smile again, his tobacco-stained fingers, the way he drank his ale with relish. But Black, the young man who rammed the pipe into the corpse's mouth and laughed… no, we never laid eyes on him again.

I will tell it to you as he did to me.

It was a cold Christmas night, but blessedly dry, and Black left the chop house brimming with anxiety. Black fancied himself as a magnanimous loser, paying his debts with a flourish and purchasing drinks for the whole party. He wanted none of us to guess the truth of his upbringing or the things he had to do to keep his brothers and himself fed. On foot, he left the dissolute district of low eateries and headed towards the more pleasant shops and promenades a few minutes' walk away. Traipsing unnoticed amongst the evening couples and costermongers, Black saw his mark. A man of forty or thereabouts, smartly tailored, walking without purpose. Indeed, he moved with the uncertainty of one who did not wish to return home until absolutely necessary. Ideal.

The shops were teeming with people searching for the perfect last minute gift. Black had no time to admire the festive windowfronts or savour the perfume of hot chestnuts and coffee. He was following his mark with the stealthy leisure of a cat. When the man paused outside a confectioner's shop, looking in at the marzipans and chocolates arranged in the window like a jewellers' counter, Black hung back and studied the man's face for signs of suspicion. Black had never seen someone so miserable at the sight of such sweet delights. He clearly had the means to go inside and buy. How could one so affluent be so unappreciative? Black felt a knot of resentment tighten around his gut.

As a gaggle of shop girls and their beaus tramped gaily by, Black had the distraction he needed; striding alongside them, his fingers dipped easily into the man's pocket, touched coin, and slipped out. He moved on with easy speed, disappearing as quickly as the girls and their admirers. The man continued to stare mournfully at the peppermint creams, having felt nothing.

Black walked a safe distance around the back of Saint Timothy's church before taking stock of his earnings. Strangely, there were no coins in the pocket where he stuffed them. He could have sworn he felt metal at the crucial moment, but no. Numb with cold, his fingers touched card. He took the thing out to look at it. With disappointment, he realised this was no folded banknote or pawn shop ticket. He had stolen a photograph.

He cursed. Now he would have to find another pigeon and take a second risk. He was about to toss the picture over the graveyard wall when its subject caught his eye. It was a child. Aged five at most. She sat dozing in a chair surrounded by her dolls and stuffed animals, looking to all the world like a little lady in her striped frock and buckled shoes. Clutched in her small fist was a sprig of holly, and Black with his physician's eyes recognised the tell-tale discolouration creeping in at the fingertips. Black turned the photograph over.

Florabelle's last Christmas.

Black wiped his face. A daughter, sadly departed. The photograph was useless to him, of no value at all, but to the man he had stolen it from? Florabelle's father, presumably. To have lost the child at

Christmas, and then lost what could well be his only visual record of her… All for the want of ten shillings. Black felt sick.

Well, he shouldn't have been carrying it with him, the idiot. What did he expect to happen? Black would never have taken it had he known what it was. Damned strange it was, too, when he could have sworn he touched coin. The poor fellow would simply have to go back to the photography studio and ask about another copy. Surely they had the means to produce such a thing.

But the photograph could have been taken years ago. Would the studio retain originals after so much time? And then there was the anguish the man would surely feel when he got home and removed his overcoat only to realise a familiar hard rectangle was missing from his pocket. It was easy to imagine him fumbling with mounting panic, retracing his steps, going out into the cold night with pluming breath, peering at the cobbles for the slightest sign of poor, lost Florabelle.

There was no choice but to return it.

Florabelle's father had not gone far. He was a long string of a man, and Black could see him in the distance, walking with more purpose now that the temperature was dropping. Black picked up the pace. If he timed it right he could make the fellow believe he had dropped the photograph. Black would be a kind of hero then, perhaps even earn himself a tip. But then, to Black's dismay, he saw his mark hail a carriage. With no money to pay a driver of his own, Black had no choice but to break into a run.

It was a mercifully short journey, but by the time the carriage stopped at a row of fine houses, Black was wheezing with exertion. He stayed out of sight, the child's picture in his hand, and watched as her father reluctantly dismounted the carriage. Florabelle had tripped along these pavements and played in these gardens. She had most likely taken her last breath in that house. Black felt renewed self-reproach.

The gentleman rang his bell and was admitted by a servant. When they were safely inside, Black resolved to slide the photograph through the letterbox and make his escape. He stole up the path, praying the poor lamplight would hide his face from any curious neighbours. He was poised at the door when he noticed the servant had left it ajar.

The house was decked out for Christmas. He could smell dinner cooking and feel the friendly warmth of log fires and gaslight. It was no longer a house in mourning, but nevertheless Black perceived the fossilised heaviness of the place, a hollow imprint where once a small life had taken up space.

A strange compulsion took hold of Black. He went inside.

"Excuse me... I say, don't be alarmed, sir, but you dropped something..."

He expected the servant to come running. Florabelle's father must have retired to his room upstairs, and his wife, whose feminine trappings Black noticed here and there, was nowhere to be seen. He thought to lay the photograph on a side table and leave, but that perverse impulse to stay only increased when no servant came. Black called out again, half hoping no one would answer him as he gingerly opened the door to the little sitting room. A modest Christmas tree decorated with candies and ribbons was set off to one side, and Black found himself thinking that Florabelle would have loved the sight of it in the lamplight, glistening and fragrant. He could almost imagine her small form standing beside the tree, reaching up to touch.

What was he doing? He had broken into this house, more or less, and was standing there witlessly, waiting for a servant to discover him with a scream. He hastened to the mantlepiece and placed the photograph in the centre, standing up so it would easily be found.

"There," he said, feeling like a fool for it. "You're home."

The lights went out.

Black swore. Something was wrong with the gas. The residents would surely come to investigate and find him there, lurking in the darkness like a murderer. As his eyes adjusted to the darkness, Black found the door and opened it, going back out into the hall as quietly as he could manage.

Was it the hall? The lights had been extinguished all over the house. Black was disorientated. The front door had seemed so close to the sitting room, but now he found he couldn't see it. It had only been a few paces away, but when he took those steps now Black found he had taken a wrong turning into the dining room. The long table was set out with unlit candles and sprays of greenery, jagged in the dark. Black turned back. To his confusion, he had to open a door to get back out into the hall. He couldn't recall opening one to enter the dining room. Still, it was terribly difficult to see, and the effort of making no sound, plus the knowledge that at any moment he would be discovered, had his heart pounding unhealthily.

Black put his arms out in front of him. Something jangled as took a step. Utensils swinging in his face. With a sharp intake of breath, Black realised he had wandered into the kitchen. The kitchen! There was no one inside, thank heavens, and Black stood for a moment, bewildered at how he had ended up there. He had been drinking, he reminded himself. As he turned to retrace his steps, he pushed open a door, and with his hand on the doorknob he realised once again that he had no memory of opening it seconds before. Worse, he found himself at the foot of the servant's stairs. He knew he had walked down no such flight. Panic took root. There was nowhere to go but up the stairs, two at a time, and through the door at the top, leading out into—

A bedroom. Yes, that was a bed before him, clear in the moonlight. A dressing table, a wash basin, a book lying by the pillow. Black's shaking hand grasped the doorknob and he backed out onto the stairs, staring stupidly. It was no trick of the darkness. The stairs had vanished, and in front of him was another door. He hardly dared touch it, but he had no other choice. There was no excuse under the sun that allowed for his presence outside a stranger's bedroom in the chill December night. They hanged burglars, didn't they? And hanged men so frequently found their way onto student's dissecting tables.

Door. A nursery. Door. Another bedroom. Door. The dining room again with its candles and greenery. There was a noise coming from somewhere outside the house. A hailstorm had started up. The skies had been clear and fresh, he was sure of it. And that moonlight was unimpeded by clouds mere minutes ago. But it was unmistakable – he could hear the windows rattle under a barrage of icy pellets.

As he stumbled through room after room, the storm gathered strength. The roof was pelted hard. The noise of it cut through any remaining composure Black possessed. He was lost. It was hopeless. All around him, that terrible clattering, on the ceilings and windows and that unreachable front door like bullets against a tin hut. Black felt small blows on his arms and back, but in his panicked brain still a speck of reason prevailed – loud noise, darkness, a trick of the mind, nothing can hurt you here, you only *believe*…

A small, hard object hit him on the chin. Black cried out in horror.

The floor was alive with rolling objects threatening to trip him. Pebbles? Marbles? He plunged through door after door. Kitchen, parlour, withdrawing room, bedroom, kitchen once more, and in his bewilderment Black began to weep. He broke into a run, charging headlong through door after door until there was no interval between them, merely an endless blockade of wood cascading open before him. The house was a vindictive thing, contorting and reforming itself with the single intention of tormenting Black.

"I surrender! I'm sorry. I returned the picture. I'm heartily sorry. What do you *want?*"

With that final word, Black's descent came to an end. He stood panting in the little sitting room with the Christmas tree and the last embers of the fire dying in the grate. The clattering ceased. The clock ticked, and when he moved his feet there were no pebbles or marbles on the floor to hinder them. The photograph of Florabelle rested on the mantelpiece where he left it. Her eyes were closed, but Black would later swear he felt himself appraised.

But not from the mantelpiece. The sensation made him turn and squint at the foot of the Christmas tree. Something was trailing along the carpet. Aghast, Black watched as it gathered shape and mass. This was no trick of the optic nerve, no product of an overworked liver. Black was alone with a mist becoming fog becoming smoke becoming flesh, so dense and real he could have reached out and held the little stiff hand with its proffered sprig of holly.

Black was incapable of articulating the terror that gripped him. With animal desperation, he hurled the only weapon he had at the spectre – a handful of lemon drops from his pocket. As he fled, he heard them clatter all around him, that now-familiar sound, followed by what could only be described as a childish gurgle of pleasure.

This time, when the sitting room door opened, it allowed him into the hall. The front door was open, the night clear and still. Black pelted out into the cold. Featherstone never did see his ten shillings.

I would barely have given Black's story any credence had I not paid a Christmas Eve visit to Carrington's Confectioners at Queen Street. I was after some sugarplums for the girl I was courting and took note of a well-heeled gentleman speaking to the proprietor in hushed but excited tones. Had anyone lately purchased a large quantity of lemon drops? Only: "They were my little girl's favourites. She has been dead a year, and my wife and I – well, this season is brutally hard on us both. Forgive me. The lemon drops. They were my daughter's favourite. And last night, she – someone – the most extraordinary thing – when we woke this morning, our house was full of them. Every room, every surface. Like a child's dream."

In answer to your question, yes. I do believe the dead communicate. They have their ways.

|Cremating Imelda|

Imelda never asked to be cremated, but it was too late to say anything now.

Her brother, Russell, understood the delicacy of the situation. "A coffin of that size is a big deal. I mean, if I can be honest, Kate, they don't make 'em that wide. That's bespoke. And think of the pallbearers. We can give her a plaque in the garden, maybe a little pond. She'd like that. Being outside again."

Kate was the closest thing to a nurse Imelda would allow in their bungalow on the Norfolk coast. Solemn Kate, better acquainted than Imelda would like with E45 and webcams and the torpid flow of strangers: American, Dutch, Senegalese. Faceless freaks, Kate called them. None of this was her fault. On the morning of the funeral, Kate took her mother's gold cross and hung it by its chain over the mirror in the hallway. It would have slipped off her shoulders had she put it on.

When her cremation began, Imelda couldn't see much of the action. For one thing, the corrugated cardboard box they'd put her in squashed the spill of her upper arms into the hanging folds of her separated bosoms like dimpled mounds of cheese, but she was used to such inconveniences. What confused her was the sudden temptation to move. Not physically, obviously, although the first flush of flame had a lively effect on the tendons deep inside the hillocks of her knees. No, Imelda was aware of a change in the rules. There was a... I beg your pardon? A treat was coming.

Treats were harmful things. People were always telling Imelda that. They thought she didn't listen. But Imelda was good at listening. Her unique situation meant she saw little of the outside world beyond the old fridge rusting in the garden she vaguely remembered standing in, once. As she lay in bed, feeling the fluctuating temperatures of the passing seasons, Imelda's other senses had learned to compensate.

Her hearing swelled to encompass seagulls and dog walkers, Tesco delivery vans and dustmen, and the clattering of the far-off spinnakers as they turned to catch the headwinds. In the end, Imelda thought she could hear the drone of the listless clouds in the cold Norfolk sky, but that may have been the kitchen light.

Yes, she had stood in the garden with Daniel, yonks ago. Her wedding band still fit her finger then. "I want fireworks at my funeral," Daniel told her, looking out over the sea. "Bright loud bangs."

Russell conceded only to an indoor sparkler on a black forest gateau. "There's nothing to celebrate, 'Mel. He's gone."

The years dragged. The rest of the community took their belongings and drove off on account of the sea's slow consumption of the cliffs. One little house over the edge, then the next. The tongues of the sea, lapping, insatiable.

Now, in the crematorium, Imelda used what was left of her ears. The nice young man whose job it was to press the button made a high-pitched sound, and it intrigued her. Surely you'd need a stronger set of nerves for a job like—

"Shit," he said. "Shit."

Imelda sighed into the shelf of her double chin. In its fiery cocoon, her body swelled slightly. It was only a small sin, swearing, but one more for her to deal with. What would Father Green have said?

"God helps those who..." et cetera. But God had not helped Imelda, despite creating and allegedly loving all four-hundred-and-forty pounds of her. They had workmen for that, in the end. Father Green had kept up his weekly visits as they took down the bedroom wall from the outside and pinned up a blue tarpaulin for modesty. He was a sensitive man. All those telephoto lenses. The laughing boys on bikes. *Why don't you* do *something?* he was always thinking, though he knew she could hear. *There are exercises for the bedridden. Stop these horrid displays. Consider a gastric band. Please, Imelda.*

And underneath, in the chamber of his mind, the animals. Whale. Hippo. Sow.

She cast her mind back to the sight of him perching on the plastic garden chair propping open the bedroom door. Nowhere else to put it – the room was *all* bed, a tremendous reinforced thing that, like her, was neither attractive nor comfortable. She remembered him wondering where her skeleton was, floating inside that reservoir of fat. Imelda supposed it was only natural. They proceeded with their business.

"Our first case today is one of theft. Theft of…" he paused sensitively, "food."

Imelda needed a name.

"Ah, no – that isn't how it works, Imelda. The confession is an anonymous forum. A conversation between God and the penitent. I'm just the operator."

Imelda needed a name. That was how it worked.

Father Green never did get over the shame of breaking a confidence. "Dominic Graham, twenty-eight. Works on the deli counter at Sainsbury's. He, ah… sometimes takes a slice of ham and scoffs it on his break."

Imelda asked for the variety of ham.

"I didn't think to ask."

It was the kind with peppered edges. Imelda could easily process this sin. She tongued each pink, peppery lump of it, Dominic's salty guilt clinging to it in crystals that smashed like diamonds between her teeth. All washed down with the certainty of forgiveness; the creamiest, frothiest milk of The Holy Mother. A slow nod to Father Green: it was taken care of. He let out a long sigh, deflating with relief.

Father Green had been coming to the bungalow every Thursday since Imelda's talent had become apparent, around the time she became too large to leave the bed. Imelda was glad of the company, walled up in her bedroom like an anchoress. Russell left brochures for Kate – dreary little care homes down Yarmouth way. But how does one go about evicting a woman large enough to roll over and squash Norfolk County Council? As the roads into the village became clogged with weeds and the streetlights winked out, Imelda knew, like dear old Daniel, that she would never leave alive.

Kate cried when they made the decision to stay. She hated the waves crashing below the garden, little bites getting bigger each night. *Just go*, Imelda would say. *I love you.*

"Listen to you. Always got to be the martyr."

Imelda had listened during her funeral. Russell, puffed up with embarrassment like a nasty spot, gave a speech. He'd brought a carload of the mini Scotch eggs she liked, for afterwards. Years ago, he warned her people would come to gawp. Now he felt responsible.

"No one with a camera gets a Scotch egg. No, none of you. Alright?"

People will cross continents if you give them something worth staring at.

Still, before the end, Father Green cycled out to the cliffs every Thursday. At the conclusion of each session, Kate would shuffle in with her laptop, her webcam and a big bag of cheesy Wotsits.

"Right, your Holiness, I'm turfing you out. It's five o'clock on the East Coast now, Mum. Your creeps are waiting."

Gorge-ous Gretel, at Queen of Greed dot com. Imelda disliked the name Gretel, and had said so in the beginning. She said so now, in front of Father Green.

"That's all part of it, Mum. You're tapping into childhood fantasies. It's the id. Manipulate the id and you've got them."

Kate, the cleverest girl Imelda knew. The money helped her through community college where incapacity benefit never could. And so, every second night, Imelda crammed fist after fist of orange Wotsits into her mouth for the titillation of two-dozen men whose radiating self-loathing was like sand down the long chute of her throat.

The boys on bikes said it was Imelda who was making the cliffs collapse. Specifically her fucking massive freakshow arse. Their sins were hard to swallow, slimy-thorny, that rotten vice of pleasure derived from the suffering of others. It lingered after Wotsits, Mr Kipling Cherry Bakewells, even the giant Christmas Toblerones that usually solved everything.

Jesus had cheekbones sharp as the breakers on a February morning. Her fingers orange with cheesy dye as she tipped the upturned bag into her mouth, Imelda wondered how the Lord would hide his revulsion when the time came.

An alarm wailed.

The nice young man cursed and stumbled. Imelda strained to make it out, but the roar of the flames became louder, as powerful as she imagined aeroplanes to be, ready to take all those lucky holidaymakers somewhere wonderful and warm.

He yelled. Imelda would suggest he have a nice sugary cup of tea and some custard creams; that takes the edge off for her. But his colleagues had come running at the sound of the alarm, and they were swearing too. Imelda realised her too-small cardboard enclosure had gone. Aah. Better.

As Father Green left the bungalow that last time to watch the evening tides change along the cliffs, he swept a look over the immense mammalian mass of her, sprinkled with the leavings of those damned orange Wotsits.

"It's never too late, Imelda. Remember what Christ said to the fallen woman."

Go, and sin no more. Heavy, guts aching with the burden he had left her, how could she? She had to eat. She was still a living creature, no matter what they said.

Well, *was*. But she could still agitate people in death. The nice man had never seen anything like this. They had safety measures in place for this eventuality, surely, but— "What do you mean, turn it off? I've tried. It's in the vents. Shit. It's the smoke, it— Shit."

Sins, sins, sins. Imelda, supine, mouth wide to receive. Yet something was different. A strange satiety was seeping into her innermost cavities where muscle cleaved sluggishly to bone. It was not unpleasant, sliding caramel-hot down into the empty parts of her, the long labyrinth of tubing from end to end that only knew the ache of too much or too little. Beyond her chamber, the nice man and his friends had left her. The aftertaste of their small sins was confectionary to Imelda, guiltless treats to nibble and discard.

No longer hers to take.

Whoomph. A rushing sound like a downpour on the rusting fridge outside her window. Daniel said he'd get around to moving it one day. The stroke had put pay to that; then the merciless shingles gnawing their way up his spine, those had finished off his will to live. If Imelda were to allow herself one final self-indulgence in these last moments of heat and light and loneliness, it would be regret; regret for Daniel who never got his fireworks.

A bright loud bang.

She could *move*.

Firemen! Just like on the telly. Dozens of them, streaming in with fine rounded biceps and meaty thighs in heatproof overalls. Out Imelda burst from her chamber to greet them. Up in the air vents, billowing out joyously into the room, rushing down – *Hello!* – as they waded through the clinging miasma. She embraced them, coated them, slinking around the crook of knees and the sweet spot between neck and shoulder. From her various vantage points, Imelda could taste them all, the individual cologne of them, this morning's soap, core temperatures lovingly preserved at thirty-six degrees. Salt on their skin; lip-smacking, bad-for-you salt. Some of them carried sins, big sins, sins larger than her body, even. But she was airborne now; fire, smoke, and hot black grease. Their sins were no longer hers to swallow.

They'd be needing a new roof. Imelda tried to recall the name of the man who'd done the patio for Daniel donkey's years ago, but the good Norfolk wind caught her and flew with her, up, away from the smoking crematorium. Imelda rode the thermals, out over flat tilled earth, barreling down over caravan parks and amusement arcades, dispersing fine white ash over the little village pubs where she shared pork scratchings with Daniel, a lifetime and four-hundred pounds ago. The cliffs were a crack between white sky and black field, and she headed for the edge with glee.

Daniel never got his fireworks. She hoped this would do.

440-pound corpse sets fire to crematorium.

Investigators believe that the mid-November blaze in Norfolk began when large amounts of burning fat from a four-hundred-and-forty-pound woman's body blocked an air filter, which in turn caused the filter system to overheat, Anglia News reports.

"Bodies of this size are a modern phenomenon," Chief Firefighter Martin Briggs told the media. "New facilities must be created to process them."

Father Green averted his eyes from the demolition's final throes. A small television crew had turned up to watch the JCB push the last of Imelda's bungalow into the swiftly encroaching sea. A preventative measure, they called it, though the sightseeing children had long since found other distractions inland.

In days gone by, women like Imelda were honoured grandmothers, traveling midwives, cunning folk of dreadful, wondrous influence. Father Green had his wooden box with the grill through which the faceless congregation confessed, but he knew all those voices, and they all knew him, and it was so terribly weighty, so hard to digest. He tucked his chin into his scarf and watched a Wagon Wheel wrapper blow over the cliff.

"Thank you, Imelda. I shall come again next Thursday."

Along the coast, Imelda took a gasp of briny air. The sea has no sins.

|The Cherry Cactus of Corsica|

"I feel I don't know Joshua very well," Kurt said.

Henry Wismer examined the schnapps on Kurt's desk. If his son had been caught glugging Dom Pérignon on college property, Kurt got the feeling Mister Wismer wouldn't be quite so dismayed. Uncomfortable in silence, even Skype silence, Kurt looked at the man's dextrous hands and imagined them around the rare orchid he vaguely remembered him cradling at the Chelsea Flower Show. The long nails were a surprise. But Kurt supposed the Wismer riches meant he personally never had to come within a metre of actual soil.

Of all the difficult aspects of teaching, parental interaction was the worst. Somehow it was worse on a laptop screen. Kurt would have to coax him. "Has Josh done this sort of thing before?"

Mister Wismer offered him nothing. No, then. Kurt felt for them both. Josh was a good student. Consciously, consistently good. All that hard work and all those manners built up in an eighteen-year-old body like steam. When Kurt found Josh gulping cherry schnapps in the common room after final bell, he had only been surprised for a second.

Wismer took his eyes off the garish pink bottle. "What are your disciplinary procedures?"

Detention was hard to enforce at sixth form. They knew they didn't have to be there. "I just felt you ought to know."

"Alcohol is not something our family tolerates. I'm sorry. What with Joshua starting mid-term, you've hardly had time to get to know him. Or me."

"Josh said he's been to many schools."

Josh had said almost nothing at all, in fact, like any boy who never stayed anywhere long enough to bother making friends. Kurt understood. He had been a shy kid, too.

"I design gardens," Wismer said. "Travel is a necessity. My company cultivates some of the rarest specimens in the world, and the demand is high. Monthly meetings with collectors take preparation, and Josh is usually so good at taking care of himself, I'm guilty of letting him get on with it. I'd like to say it would have been different with his parents, but they had a similar lifestyle."

"I'm sorry. I thought you were Josh's dad."

"My sister and her husband passed away when Joshua was young. I took him on, and his brother. Have you met Shane? About the same age as you."

Kurt recalled a sullen young man leaning on a nice car, watching Josh scuff his way across the carpark at last bell. One of the girls said he was Josh's boyfriend, and that was it, he was officially the fruitiest faggot who ever lived. It was probably the same for him everywhere.

Quiet kids. It took time to bring them round, and time wasn't a luxury teachers had. Pouring himself a shot of schnapps in front of the TV that night, Kurt nonetheless decided Josh was worth the effort.

"You can go when your brushes are clean, and *only* when they're clean."

Kurt washed the paint off his hands as B13 filed out, noisily ignoring him. For all his talk of cleanliness, he'd managed to get acrylic in his hair. The room was silent by the time Kurt had picked out the worst of it, so he was startled when he turned from the mirror to see Josh still at his desk, unpacking his lunch from his rucksack.

"Is it alright if I eat here? I know it's not really allowed."

It was the privacy Josh wanted, and Kurt couldn't begrudge him that. In the Tupperware box on his lap was a salad of spinach leaves and what looked like slices of rare steak. Kurt had eaten Coco Pops for breakfast and took two sugars in his coffee. He'd never seen a healthier teenager. It wasn't natural, but Kurt had to admit, Joshua didn't have spots.

Josh sipped his juice. Some kind of horrendous smoothie, magenta with flecks of green.

"Your uncle didn't give you too hard a time?"

Josh didn't look up. "Sorry for being stupid. I wasted his evening. And yours."

Kurt had expected something sarcastic about being sent down the mines. He watched the boy stab a few spinach leaves with his fork, chewing them with conscious purpose.

"You'll grow up big and strong." Kurt cringed at himself. He was in danger of calling him 'son'. He was relieved to notice Josh's sketchbook open on the desk. He'd been working on something, a village of huddled rooftops emerged from a few cursory lines. "This is good."

"I can never get it right."

"There you go – a proper artist. You hate your own stuff."

A diffident smile under a curtain of soft hair. Josh closed the sketchbook. This was the boy Kurt had found in the common room after everyone else had gone home, taking grimacing mouthfuls of schnapps like it was the antidote to a fast-acting poison. Now, he wiped the rim of his smoothie bottle with his thumb, then wiped his thumb on a fresh tissue. Kurt had an idea.

"Do some more on it tonight. Then come and show me, okay?"

He didn't come the next day, or the next week. Kurt saw him long enough each morning to take his name for the register, but after that Josh was only ever shouldering his bag and slinking off. He seemed okay, despite some of the Year 12 girls ramping up the gossip. They saw him filing his nails, they said. Who does that? And what kind of boy brings raw spinach for lunch – every day, by all accounts?

It was a month since the schnapps incident when Kurt found him in the common room, standing at his locker. He could smell the wine.

"It's after home-time," Josh panted, like that made it all fine, but he only let go of the bottle when Kurt took it from him.

"Josh. I know some of the others are making your life difficult. But you've got so much going for you. You could go to university. Maybe study abroad."

Josh wiped his mouth with the back of his hand. "I had a maths tutor in Paris. I took an introduction to architecture in Glasgow. I learned to waltz on a ship from Ireland to America. Wasn't long enough, I'm terrible." He stared up at Kurt, eyes hazy with aimless frustration. "It's an experiment."

Kurt took Josh and his experimental bottle to the staff room. The coffee machine beeped. Kurt poured two strong cups before pouring the wine down the staff room sink. Josh looked at the clock on the wall, the coffee steaming away in front of him.

"How's your drawing coming along?"

"It's not finished." Josh was sullen, but still produced the sketchbook for Kurt to peruse.

"Those cactuses are great. You've really captured the texture."

"*Opuntia prunus-indica,*" Josh said. "My dad was a botanist."

"Runs in the family, then?"

"No."

He'd sketched a landscape, a Riviera scene with mountains pouring down into a sparkling twilight sea. A domed church dominated the foreground, and down the mountainside, roads zigzagged into a tumbledown village. He was extraordinary, this kid. He must have studied art along the way – really studied it, not the painting-by-numbers crap Missus Priestley drummed into them over in the high school.

"Mum sketched," Josh said. "She taught me."

"Your uncle must be pretty pleased with you."

The boy looked at the sink where the least dregs of wine clotted red around the plughole. "My old form tutor, at the last place, she was very encouraging."

"Yeah?" Kurt took a packet of sugar and made a show of shaking it into his coffee. He was doing the chummy voice again. It made him nervous to listen to himself.

"Miss Faith," Josh said. "Kind of funny. She was an RE teacher."

Just then, a rap at the door made Josh jump. Through the frosted glass, Kurt saw the shape of someone tall and distinctly pissed off. The door swung open before Kurt could get off the couch.

"Can I help you?"

"You're actively hindering me, actually." A young man pushed past and presented himself to Josh. "Hello. Do you remember me? I'm the one with the car."

Josh was already hurrying to put his things away. The lunchbox with the remnants of spinach leaves clattered out of his bag onto the floor. "He kept me behind."

"Did he arrest you? Were you shackled to that chair?"

So this was Shane. With his leather jacket and blonde hair groomed like a showdog's, Josh's brother had that same clear-skinned gymnastic look to him, with none of the wholesomeness.

Kurt held out his hand and found the empty wine bottle thrust into it.

"You're the form tutor, aren't you?" Shane demanded. "What is the point of you? If you can't keep one boy from harming himself in your care, why pay your pitiful salary at all?"

Okay, wow, straight to the sore spot. Kurt placed the wine bottle well behind him where it couldn't be broken over his head.

"Perhaps now isn't the best time to have a chat," he said in the confrontation-deflecting voice his colleagues said made him sound like someone's mum. "But it'd be really—"

Shane made a face. "We're needed at home. But I am far from done with you."

As Josh was herded out into the corridor, Kurt wondered who 'you' was.

Kurt turned to the schnapps before he could sleep. He told himself he'd had too many coffees at work, but it was Shane's face he saw when he turned off the bedside light. When Kurt thought of Mister Wismer's contrasting coolness he tried to imagine himself in Josh's place, traipsing around the world between those two personalities.

The schnapps was foul, but he drank it gladly, in bed with the muffled sounds of his neighbours in the flats either side of him. No chance of sleep, and he knew it.

Teenagers drink. Kurt had been no different at Josh's age, though he really only did it to blend in. Josh drank alone, and that was a big distinction, but if he was developing a problem, surely he'd be at it every week, every day. This monthly public binge was more like a cry for help. But why make a gesture like that and still come in every day with lunch like something from a Californian detox retreat?

Josh was eighteen. He wasn't a child in need of protection. He wasn't a vulnerable adult, either, by strict definition. Those channels of help were closed to him. But Shane was right, Kurt had a duty of care.

His brain hummed with the few words he'd exchanged with Josh since meeting him. Miss Faith the RE teacher. He'd met a Miss Faith at a conference. They'd flirted a little and he made the obvious joke about her being a crucial member of her department. They'd talked long enough to learn where she worked and parted company without too much awkwardness.

But what would he say? A student you've probably forgotten has done two mildly naughty things in as many months? He could just hear her in the staff room afterwards: *'This rando I met once came up with an excuse to call me…'*

Kurt went to the window. Down in the street, someone in a dressing gown was struggling to turn off their car alarm while a pair of boys straddling bikes laughed. Josh would be at home – wherever home for the Wismer family was these days – in a bed paid for by rare orchids from countries Kurt could never afford to visit. Not on the salary Shane so rightly sneered at. Josh would be fine. A little lonely, a little nervous, but when had that done anyone any real damage?

And then he found himself thinking about the other men sleeping in that house tonight. No mother, no sisters, no aunts. The missing women disturbed him in some indefinable way. And when he thought of Josh sitting alone with his steak and his smoothie, Kurt wanted him to be happy, and normal, and safe.

Safe.

He put down his drink and opened his laptop.

"I'm calling about a student of mine. He used to be yours, he recently transferred, and I'm… well, it's Joshua. Joshua Wismer."

"Doesn't ring a bell."

Shit. Okay. Could he have the wrong Miss Faith? "He probably wasn't with you for very long, so…"

On the end of the line, the woman audibly sighed. "Then I can't really help you."

"But you could. You could. If you remember having a student, rather shy, longish brown hair, likes to draw…" Kurt felt sweat prickle in the hollows of his palms. It was stupid to call her. He didn't even know what he was asking.

"You're describing every teenager I've ever met."

"Spinach and steak."

And she paused. "What?"

"He always has it for lunch. With this horrible pink concoction. You know him, don't you?"

In the background he could hear someone enter the office, ask a question, then leave. Only then did Miss Faith speak. "His name wasn't Joshua. Is he well? Of course he's not. Why would you be calling me if he was okay?"

Kurt realised his heartrate had picked up. "Sorry, did you just say he was under a different name?"

"Daragh. Daragh with the weird diet." She breathed into the speaker, holding it too close. "Has his brother done something?"

"Shane?"

"Shit."

Kurt's second coffee of the morning turned to acid in his stomach. "Shane's not his name, is it?"

"Charlie," she said, with audible distaste. "Creepy Charlie. 'Charlie's harmless', Daragh told me, with this look on his face, like he was talking about a great white shark. He was chatting up girls in the carpark while he waited for Daragh. We're attached to the High School, so *young* girls, telling them he'd take them for a spin. I put a stop to him coming inside the gates."

"What can you tell me about Daragh?"

"What is it now, 'Joshua'? He was pretty unremarkable. Bullied. Some of the kids found out he had a public Twitter under a silly name, posting all sorts of weird stuff. I had to intervene in the end. He begged me not to tell his uncle. Almost cried on me. He was so grateful, Daragh. He didn't talk about uni or a career or any of it, but he was so thankful to be here… It chimed wrong with me. Like he thought it could all be taken away at any moment."

"Did you meet his uncle?"

"No. When Daragh was ill, Charlie would call in sick for him. I assume he did most of the parenting. He sent him off with those weird lunches."

"Was he ill often?"

"Pretty much every month. He'd need a few days off. He never got behind on work. Somehow, he always had it all taken care of before he got sick. I don't get why it happened so often. Not with the way he took care of himself."

When he imagined Shane filling that Tupperware box every morning with rare beef cut in perfect squares, Kurt somehow couldn't bring himself to tell her about the drinking. Creepy Charlie. Josh's desperate eyes and the smell of cheap wine. *It's an experiment.* The words hadn't made an impression on him at the time, but now he wanted nothing more than to hang up the phone and go and pull Josh out of whatever class he was quietly sitting in.

"Do you remember the name he was tweeting under?" he asked.

"Yes, actually," Miss Faith said. "'Flask'. I said to him at the time, 'Is the flask half full or half empty?', trying to lighten him up a bit, you know. And he just stared at me. He was always so serious, Daragh."

"Joshua."

"Whoever he is."

Kurt waited until he was at home with his own computer to go trawling Twitter. It wasn't a world he was familiar with, putting one's feelings out in the open for anyone to get at. He had to scroll through hundreds of usernames, so many profile photos of pouting teenage boys that he had to pour a glass of schnapps to focus. It was a quarter to midnight and that car alarm was going off again when he found him.

Flask. It was Josh's face, alright, the same as if he'd taken the picture that morning.

No wonder he was so hard to find. He had no likes, and as good as no followers. Just one picture remained. It was Josh's drawing. A rocky Mediterranean hillside rolling down into a village. Clumps of bulbous cacti like bloodshot eyes, and an old horse-drawn carriage labouring down the hill, touched by the moonlight.

He'd called it *The Cherry Cactus of Corsica.*

Kurt sat back in his chair. Josh had posted the drawing the previous night. It was a perfect piece of pencil landscape work, verging on the sort of photorealism an artist might hope to master late in his career. For all his worrying, Kurt felt a resurgence of second-hand pride at the boy's talent, his striking use of colour in an otherwise monochrome composition.

The sea was a rusty copper-tang red.

Kurt struggled to sleep. It was probably his new habit of a drink before bed. More than a tipple, really, but he told himself when he finished the schnapps he could throw the bottle out and stop having to look at it.

3:23am. He was going to be good for nothing at work tomorrow. And for what? Sitting up and staring at a tweet.

When his flat's buzzer went, he thought it was morning, that he had drifted off and was late for work. The room was dark, all but the intrusion of the streetlights, and the buzzer yelled and yelled. Kurt pulled on a hoodie and shuffled to the door. He put his face to the peep hole.

The motion-sensing hallway light had always been sluggish, so there was a second of darkness before Shane materialised in a florescent halo. Blonde hair and bored eyes. Kurt was still half-asleep. Opened the door with muscle memory only. Shane had a potted plant and gave it to Kurt before he had a chance to ask what he was doing there in the middle of the night.

"In central Africa, the locals offer cuttings of plants from their own gardens as a sign of contrition."

Kurt's eyes were tacky for want of water. He rubbed at them as the cactus came into focus, bristling with pernicious prongs. "It's lovely."

"It's hallucinogenic if you smoke it, so there's that."

"This is… late."

"Is it?" Shane asked, flippantly oblivious. "Look, my uncle nagged me into this. I'm rude. Always have been. He usually finds it endearing, but when the little petal is involved, he gets protective."

They were together in the kitchen. In the flats opposite, lights were coming on as people on night shifts arrived home.

"I came here to persuade you to just…" Shane waved his hand. "Move on? We won't be staying long anyway. Our family doesn't tolerate alcohol. If you must know, Josh's parents died in a coach accident. Driver was plastered."

"I thought you were brothers?"

Shane shrugged. "Twenty-first century family."

He plonked himself down on the only kitchen chair while Kurt stood there in his hoodie and shorts, shifting from one foot to another, *sleep awake sleep awake.*

"Listen," Kurt said. "I have concerns."

"Do you."

"Boys will listen to an older brother more readily than their parents or guardians. Josh is just…"

"He's being a little shit. Not just to you. He disrupted Uncle's seminar last month. He's done it again now. I've never met such an ungrateful child."

Kurt was offended on Josh's behalf. "I've met a few."

"When I was his age, I had a job. I was relied on. I worked *hard*. He doesn't have to do anything. That's the problem. Uncle treats him like an exotic specimen, but when it's his time to behave and put other people first…"

"Have you had problems with him before?"

"No. Which makes this all the more irritating. Our uncle had to let people down. Important people."

"What does he actually do, your uncle? I mean, I know it's botany, but the everyday ins and outs of it, you know?"

Shane stared at him. His expression of bored irritation hadn't changed, but Kurt felt a sickly sensation in the pit of his gut, as if they were in a car together and had just gone too fast on a tight bend. The dull subconscious voice that told him he was hungry or needed to pee – it whispered it to him. He didn't want to know what Mister Wismer did.

"You ought to get a cleaner in once a week," Shane remarked, picking a scrap of lint from the cuff of his leather jacket.

Yes, he ought. Kurt looked around at his private chaos of homework and dirty dishes and felt a drowsy bump of alarm. It was so late. Here was this stranger. But his bed was so comfortable and his sheets so cool, he didn't mind, not really.

Bed. Pillow. Alone. Kurt rolled onto his back. He was in his underpants and he hadn't removed his contacts before sleep. Gritty.

He checked his phone. Four minutes until his regular alarm. His head ached with a taste of sleep, tantalising yet not enough. He shuffled out to the kitchenette, thinking of nothing but coffee, and was pouring water into the cafetiere when he noticed the terracotta pot waiting by the microwave. His eyes were dry, and he had to squeeze them shut and open wide to make out the card beside the plant, a folded slip of paper with ornamental cursive, so pretty as to be contemptuous.

Looking after something this uncommon takes work. Feed it, talk to it, understand how it works. Only then will it give you something worthwhile in return.

It lasted a month, the plant, and showed no signs of going anywhere. For Kurt, that had to be a record. Awkward little nuggety thing. If a Wismer was going to offer Kurt a sign of contrition, it ought to have been a blue orchid or a herb that smelled of honey, not this malignant lump. And yet Kurt cared for it. He Googled cactus feed, found himself comparing brands. It gave him something to do when he came home at night.

The Lower Sixth were doing their mock exams. Kurt wondered if there had ever been a time when he'd been free to socialise, or date, or, just imagine it, read something other than teenagers' coursework.

Rene Magritte was a twentieth century Surrealist painter. His 1946 work, The Son of Man, depicts a male whose face is hidden by a green apple. Magritte explained, "Everything we see hides another thing. We always want to see what is hidden by what we see. There is an interest in that which is hidden".

Kurt dashed off a mediocre grade, an excuse to fetch a Mars Bar from the vending machine to sustain him through the next few hours of marking. Out in the common room, he saw Josh finishing up at his locker. He looked tired, but there was nothing more sinister in his hand than his lunchbox.

"When are you going to draw me something new?' Kurt offered a smile that paled when Josh did not return it. "It's good for winding down."

"Maybe you should try it, sir." There, now he smiled, just a twitch. But his eyes were hazy in his otherwise flawless face.

"I probably should. Hey, you can tell your brother I'm happy with the cactus."

"I have to get to third period." Josh's eyes flicked up, suddenly focused. "Shane visited you?"

"No, a courier delivered it. I was so tired, I forgot I'd brought it inside, so it was two surprises in one. It was nice."

Josh took his bag and closed his locker. When Kurt could see his face again, he was blinking rapidly and Kurt had the strange impression the boy had momentarily forgotten where he was.

"What, are you going to tell me it's toxic?"

"The cactus is fine."

"It's just like the ones in your drawing. You've got something, you know? I don't think you do, actually."

A group of girls hurried noisily through the common room. They weren't the squad who had been bullying Josh, but he nonetheless tucked himself into the wall until they passed. His bag brushed the lockers, and Kurt's heart sank when he heard the clank of a glass bottle.

Anyone else would have laughed sheepishly, or offered a weak lie, but Josh opened his bag and held it up for inspection.

"20cl of gin," he said. "It's 37.5% proof. I'm eighteen. Working mothers used to dose their babies up and leave them to sleep it off."

Kurt's heart sank. "Josh. Come on, mate. I promised your brother."

"How could you promise him if he sent a courier?"

"Well, he… I mean, it was a few weeks ago…" Come to think of it, he couldn't recall the courier at his door. Just the word 'courier' growing in his mind's eye. With Josh looking up at him, something like a plea in his eyes, Kurt felt a brief, ridiculous compulsion to rush home and change the locks.

Josh shouldered his bag, went off back towards the classroom.

"I thought you had third period?"

"I forgot my flask."

Flask. The word was buried deep, and with one hint from Josh it unfurled, came shooting up into the light.

Marking could wait. When Kurt checked Twitter that night – yes, after checking the locks – the drawing of the mountain and the red sea had been deleted. He felt a prickle of anxiety as if that meant something, as if it had ever meant something in the first place.

Be calm, he told himself. A drink. All he had in the cupboards was a dribble of Bailey's left over from Christmas, but it would do the job.

When he got back to his computer, Flask's account was locked.

Kurt refreshed the page. A padlock icon and a blank feed.

"Shit. Shit." He clicked and clicked. Locked, right this moment. He wanted to shout into the screen. As he refreshed the page for the twentieth time, the lock had gone. Josh's drawing had returned, the carriage venturing down the mountainside. And a message.

Do I need to send another courier?

Ms Gale had been the Head of Sixth as long as the place had existed, and Kurt always left her office somehow feeling like one of the students. Before knocking on her door, he made certain his shirt was tucked in and his teeth were vaguely clean. He looked like a man who'd spent the night awake on the sofa, which was partially true. After reading Shane's threatening tweet – because who else could it be? – Kurt pushed his long-disused exercise bike against the door and stayed up with the snooker on until sleep took him. He'd woken with the pattern of the cushions pressed into his cheek, but also with new resolve.

"Tracey, hi. Do you have a moment? I need to talk about Josh Wismer."

She continued scrolling through emails. "You'll want to check the science lab. His uncle's there, giving a talk."

"Pardon?"

"He designs gardens for the Saudi royal family. I had no idea. He offered to come in for careers day, but Sandra's off with morning sickness, so I said, why not sooner? So he's taking first period." Ms Gale was delighted. A celebrity, here. When she eventually glanced at Kurt, she registered the fresh crop of sweat on his forehead with disappointment. "What did you want to talk about?"

"Did he say anything about me?"

"You? No." She laughed lightly. "Why would he?"

Kurt didn't run to the science lab, only because he was sweaty enough already. There was a good turn-out of students. Kurt had to crane his neck, but he couldn't make out Josh's glossy hair amongst the herd.

Instead, he saw Shane. He was sitting on a table at the back of the class, picking at his fingernails. He had a box of Wismer brand seed packs for the students, and in his leather jacket and new trainers, he looked like one himself, only from a far wealthier college.

When Kurt sat beside him, Shane continued examining his nails. "You smell ill."

"I've had a lot on my mind."

At the front of the class, Henry Wismer held court. It was the first time Kurt had seen Josh's uncle in the flesh, and he was struck by the man's lean energy. Somehow, he had been expecting someone old. Most visiting speakers were rooted to the spot by inexperience, but Mister Wismer strode freely, comfortable in front of that worst of all audiences, teenagers. As for the kids, they didn't even have their phones out. When Wismer brought up a slide on the overhead projector of a Renaissance beauty dropping belladonna into her eyes, there was an audible *'eergh'* of delight.

Wismer relished the reaction. "A plant can bring unimaginable pleasure, or excruciating pain. It may heal or maim with the slightest touch. Enhance beauty. Disfigure. Intoxicate, inebriate, invigorate, asphyxiate, one after the other, all thanks to a chain of chemicals visible only to our naked eyes as pretty green leaves. Take meadow saffron, *Colchicum autumnale*. As summer dies, it blooms in slender pink petals swaying invitingly in the grass, giving it the nickname 'naked ladies'. Charming, no? It is a poison similar to arsenic. There is no known antidote."

Kurt spoke quietly to Shane. "How did you get my address?"

"It's very rude to talk over a lecturer, you know."

"Maybe I should tweet you."

"We don't approve of social media in our family. It's vulgar."

"Where is Josh?"

Henry Wismer treated them to an image of a grinning ape in velvet livery offering a king a fluted crimson flower, its petals marbled white, like cuts of meat.

"As well as toying with our mortality," Wismer said, "plants tempt our vanity with great wealth. The tulip mania of the seventeenth century saw rational men purchase a single flower when they could have bought a house for the same price. The Calvinists of the time were moved to produce anti-tulip propaganda warning that God would strike down those greedy enough to put such prices on His gifts. And indeed He did. In due time, the plague came to those same ports where tulip bulbs were unloaded every day. With plague, princes die much the same as beggars."

Here he produced a murky painting of Dutchmen loading coffins into carts. In the ubiquitous mud, scrawny chickens scratched for scraps. No greenery could live there.

"Plants lure men with siren songs. My own great-grandfather perished in pursuit of a cactus native to the island of Corsica. Islanders claimed the cactus' sap held the secret of prolonged life. A nice story, and an excellent tourist lure, but with nature we must always be cautious. What happened to my grandfather? He went the way of the naked ladies, I suspect. Disappeared off the island, no doubt into the water." He spread his hands. "Nowadays, I wear gloves."

It was all so slick and amusing. Kurt had to remind himself why he was there.

"Where's your place in this enterprise, then, Shane?"

The young man's eyes drifted to his uncle, waving his elegant hands over a slide of an extravagant red spray of flowers. There was a small smile on Shane's face. Nothing Kurt was permitted to understand. In fact, he found himself recalling a similar look on Miss Faith's face when he had clumsily flirted with her. He thought at the time she had quite liked it.

"Botany was never much of an interest of mine," Shane said. "But that's what life is, isn't it? A series of happy accidents, if you're lucky. I only cared for the literary world. I've taken it up again in recent years. Screenplays, nothing you'll have seen. I have something new in the works, but I just can't see how it will end…"

"I want to know where Josh is."

Shane carried on as if Kurt had said nothing. "It's all about a gentleman. A most learned gentleman. Well-travelled, impeccably cultured. A diplomat of sorts. Once a month, the gentleman gathers his associates. They come in their chauffeured cars. Sometimes they fly in from France or Dubai. CEOs, Hollywood producers, minor royalty. All men, of course, because that's how it was when the gentleman began his work. When they're all comfortable in front of the fire, wined and dined, the gentleman has his assistant bring out the flask."

Kurt's shirt clung with sweat. He felt unmoored, disorientated, as if this were an unsettling dream brought on by another night spent alone on the sofa. But Shane's voice was steady, his physical presence too casually domineering to disregard.

"You're only a state schoolboy, so I can't expect you to have any grounding in alchemy, but you know what a flask is, don't you, Kurt? Scientifically speaking. For the distillation of spirits. My gentleman's flask is a little different. It bleeds."

The overhead projector clicked through to the next slide, and in the second of darkness between images, Shane's face was beautiful and deranged, his expression impossible to interpret.

"There's no violence involved. Though honestly, even if there was, the guests pay so handsomely for the privilege of meeting him, I don't expect they'd mind.

"They pay for a drop. Just a drop, taken from the thumb. One drop, in a crystal claret glass of Perrier. Presentation, always. And why do they pay for this, these men? One drop, and that's maybe all they'll ever get, for the waiting list is years long, and all visitors must be strictly vetted before handing over their thousands. Private investigators, non-disclosure agreements. My gentleman would never allow things to get out of hand. And there are dangers on both sides, of course. A newcomer can only survive a minute dose, as fresh as humanly possible. Tolerance takes time, though the rewards… well, you could barely imagine. The mind clears. Diseases are arrested. Age ceases to assault the cells. Providing you have the funds."

Unimaginable pleasure, or excruciating pain.

"What would it do for you, I wonder? Your muscles aren't up to much. Sedentary lifestyle, that. The flask's contents would stimulate those fibres. Someone might actually find you attractive. You could give Miss Faith another try."

Kurt couldn't speak. That sickening sensation of swerving at the last moment before the cliff. All he could do was sit and be subjected to Shane's insinuating whisper.

"But of course, I'm forgetting. You do know what a flask is, don't you? You've been reading up." Shane leaned in close, and a horrid thought came to Kurt that the young man might actually lick him. "He tastes so good, they call him Cherry."

Kurt's lungs had lost their substance. "You're sick."

"It's dialogue."

"Listen." Kurt fought not to stammer. "If you're involved in some kind of… something Josh isn't consenting to… it's my responsibility to step in if I think—"

Shane stretched his legs, just tickled. "If you think what? Old boy, you look like death. You go raving about Joshua looking the way you do, and you'll be sectioned."

Kurt's stood, jostling the box of Wismer seeds loudly enough that the girls in front turned around and glared. This man was enjoying his discomfort, and it roused a defiance in Kurt, unfamiliar, like too-large clothes. "I'm not afraid of you, *Charlie*."

When Kurt was a boy, he liked to draw cars. Nothing beat the sense of achievement when a few rolling lines turned into something capable of speeding away. There was nothing fancy he could do with a biro on a napkin now, but it was better than sitting staring at people in the crowded pub. If he hadn't wanted to look pathetic, he perhaps shouldn't have taken a corner table alone with his pint and crisps, but just raising his voice to order had made his palms slippery. How did all these people do it so seamlessly?

His pen turned in aimless spirals. Four weeks since Mister Wismer's presentation, and in all that time Josh's empty chair in the form room kept Kurt awake at night, alone with the residue of Shane's crooning in his ear. And Tracey Gale just accepted it! *Glandular fever, he'll be wiped out for yonks. It's terribly contagious. Are you sure you're quite well, Kurt? We worry.*

His preoccupation with the boy did nothing but roll around his brain, carving ever deeper grooves where the patterns of his own life should be. A girlfriend, a pet, a flat with thicker walls. When was the last time he visited his mum? Soon the Wismers would move on to the next city and the next college and Kurt would still be here, having done what? Acquired a cactus. The biro tore through the napkin and he pushed it aside.

The pub was filling up, and the thought of the pile of essays waiting for him at home nagged at him. Kurt drained his beer and went to stand, but found his mouth full of something unfamiliar. Pulpy-pink and overripe. Kurt spat in shock. Someone had swapped his drink while he was scribbling. Spluttering, he scanned the room and saw only laughing eyes, strangers whispering about the mess he'd made, and he had to get out, now, but the table with wet with IPA, and the fruit in his mouth was gone as quickly as it had materialised.

Words took root behind his eyes. *Josh. St Luke's. Come.*

"I'm his brother."

A lie told in a hospital was somehow much bigger than one told elsewhere. The second Kurt said it, he half-expected an enormous Polish security guard in a St Luke's gilet to rush in and flatten him, but the nurse at the desk was nothing but supportive.

"Ah, you got our message." She led him straight through the noisy waiting room and into the packed recovery bay. "We pumped his stomach, and we're replenishing his fluids. He didn't have time to absorb most of it, so that's good. We see it a lot. Don't worry."

"What happened?"

"An Ocado driver on your street found him rifling through her van this afternoon. He'd nearly finished bottle of Absolut before she caught him. Bless him, he's worried she'll be in trouble."

Josh lay on his side in the guardrailed bed, smelling sour. When he saw Kurt, his sallow face contorted with confusion.

"You shouldn't be here."

"Look at the state of you."

"Who told you I was here?"

I think you did. Kurt had raced to the hospital in a daze, the words *Josh* and *St Luke's* like thorns in his mind. He kept the troubling notion to himself as he pulled up a plastic chair. "We can talk about it later."

"No. You have to go."

The curtain was drawn aside, and a new nurse entered with a trolley. "Right, love. I just need to take some blood. I know, I don't like needles either."

"I'm used to it."

In silence, Kurt watched the nurse prepare the vials. The memory of Shane's taunting put a chill in his stomach. It was like there were leering eyes in the folds of the sterile curtains, behind the screens of the ticking monitors. When the nurse left, Josh spoke softly.

"It spoils it."

"Hey. You haven't spoiled anything."

"They don't want it… when it's like this."

A wave of nausea must have come over Josh, because he clenched his eyes shut.

"I drew the island for you, remember?" he whispered hoarsely. The stomach pump had scratched his throat, made him sound like an old man. "Shouldn't have done it. But if I don't, it… it's like none of it never happened."

It was ghastly to see him so sick and defeated. Every safeguarding Powerpoint presentation Kurt ever sat through escaped him. He had to keep it together. What was the point of him otherwise?

"Whatever happened," he said, "I need to know."

And so it came seeping out.

"We'd been staying at a villa in the hills," Josh began. "My father was a botanist. He was writing on the healing plants of Corsica. There was a folk tale. The island contained all the plants you'd need for eternal life, but no one knew the right way to combine them. He went hiking while my mother painted the views from the villa. I was bored, I suppose. I had no brothers or sisters to play with. There was another English party staying nearby, so I'd go for walks in the hope of coming across them. The housekeeper said there was a gentleman and his young friend, but they were never out in the heat of the day. She talked about 'unsavoury behaviour'. Midnight swims. Girls visiting, unchaperoned. It sounded exciting.

"My father liked to talk to strangers. Didn't care if they were lords or street sweepers, he always wanted to know everything about them. One day he returned to the villa saying he'd met a Corsican midwife who sold a potion to expecting mothers. Old recipe, based on the legend. It made them strong for the birth, she said. He bought a bottle, and she laughed, said Englishmen were her best customers lately. The unsavoury pair our housekeeper warned me about were waving money at her, trying to pry out the recipe. My father wanted to talk to them. Perhaps they were scientists too.

"I took to walking up the paths along the cliffs. Sometimes I'd sketch the horizon. When I approached some children and asked if I could take their portraits, they shied away. I knew enough French to understand what they were saying. 'Don't go with the English from the hills'."

A new patient rattled in on a gurney, surrounded by arguing family. Josh lay still, trying to stay focused.

"When I first saw Henry Wismer, the sun was behind him. I was sketching the view from the cliffs, and I felt I was being watched. It wasn't a bad feeling, but when I turned, it was like he was completely black. Just an outline with nothing inside. He said good evening, and I was so pleased to hear another English voice, I got up straight away to introduce myself. The ground was dusty, I slipped. I grabbed at something to stop from falling, but it was one of my father's stupid cacti. Sliced my hand open. Wismer came to me with a handkerchief and mopped up the blood. He was rich, I saw his clothes properly then. I told him there was no harm done and I really ought not to take up any more of his time, but he lifted my hand to his face like you might do with a lady, and he… kissed it. Kissed it where the blood was. And I wanted to pull away, but this sound came out of him, a long sigh, and…" Josh swallowed and closed his eyes. "He told me I tasted like cherries.

"They packed up and left shortly after that. The housekeeper said their villa was left looking like a tavern brawl. Broken bottles and fruit peel all over, and the local children spreading horror stories."

Kurt forced himself to nod. "But you saw him again."

"Two days later. We were returning from evening Mass, my parents and I. The priest blessed my wound, and we climbed into our carriage and set off down the mountain. It just appeared in my head, *get out*, and I did. Jumped out while we were moving. That was what saved me.

"Wismer tells everyone it was an accident. Bad roads, driver going too fast. In the beginning, he said it was bandits, which is the closest he ever got to the truth. The location changes depending on where we are and who he's talking to. Sometimes even I can't remember. And when I do, I think about leaving, how easy it would be, but there's something syrupy in my blood, and I can't remember how to book a plane ticket or make my own lunch, and without the two of them I'll just die anyway, and when I shut my eyes and try to sleep, it's 1817 and I've lost my life and no one is coming to look for me."

The machine monitoring Josh's heartrate coolly displayed the long way down from agitation to exhaustion. It broke every rule, but Kurt took Josh's hand and held it tight. He thought what a good man he'd be in a few years, with the right care. You couldn't say that very often, not unironically – a *nice young man*. But with Josh, it was true. And whatever traumatic source this fantasy sprung from, it could be dealt with.

Josh's bloodshot eyes drifted and fixed over Kurt's shoulder.

The gap between the curtains. Shane, a takeaway coffee in one hand and a bottled pink smoothie in the other.

"He's so small," Shane said, to no one.

Kurt was on his feet. His instinct was to get Shane out of the room and away from Josh before a fight could break out, but to his surprise, Shane went willingly, even meekly. Out in the relative privacy of the hall, Shane binned his untouched coffee, and the smoothie.

"I should have been there for him."

"You're here now," Kurt said. With embarrassment, he realised Shane was crying.

"Don't judge me." He had a hipflask. He took a long sip and wiped his mouth, then his eyes. "It's a lonely life. It's rich clients, temporary houses, no time to make friends. There's the money and the prestige, but what does that mean? When you can't call anywhere home."

Shane passed the flask to Kurt. He took a mouthful of cherry schnapps.

"He's going to be alright," Kurt said, handing the flask back. Horrible stuff. Salty, and spicy. Spikes through the tongue. "But right now, something is wrong. There doesn't have to be a scandal. You just need to let someone in."

"Someone like you?"

Though his eyes were wet, Shane was looking at Kurt with infuriating pity. The look of a wealthy young man convinced the struggles of others were the result of their own bumbling feebleness.

Yes, Kurt wanted to say. *Yes, little me.* But the sour schnapps had filled his mouth with saliva and he couldn't manage it.

We don't approve of alcohol in our family.

Oh.

This wasn't alcohol.

Kurt spat. Magenta droplets against the hospital tiles. He looked at Shane in anger and alarm, but the young man only shrugged.

"One drop in a glass of Perrier, and one drop only. That's the rule for guests. In alchemy, the flask itself is of limited importance. The ingredients and the distilling process is where the mystery lies, but we've combined all three. We had to experiment for years to find the perfect host. Plenty of street children in Corsica, though."

The Snickers bars in the vending machine pulsed in time with Kurt's quickening heart.

"The flask's blood is tricky," Shane said. "You can keep it hospitable with a strict diet, but if the little urchin goes and sabotages all my hard work with a bottle of WKD, nothing can be done. Have you any idea how frustrating that is?"

In the busy corridor, staff and patients passed them by without a second glance.

"I can't feel my face." Kurt blinked, trying to clear his vision. With a surge of panic, he imagined Shane had slipped him LSD, or ketamine, or any one of the recreational drugs Kurt had never been sociable enough to try. He had to shout for help, he told himself. This was a hospital. Shane only meant to frighten him. Kurt felt the wall bump against his back, icy cold. His lips, he noticed with alarm, were slack and unresponsive.

"You know what his life is like, at home?" Shane was intimately close now. Kurt could only gape at his skin, pristine with youth. Creepy Charlie. "Twenty-four hour luxury, right from the beginning. He isn't chained up in a cellar. That doesn't work. You have to let them be a little independent, or they turn stale. We had dribblers, in the beginning. Basement troglodytes. It's unworkable. The process has arrested Joshua's body and mind at eighteen years old, or thereabouts, and that's ideal. Still malleable. A twenty-year-old is too much to handle, and children are a nightmare. Joshua is altogether a perfect rarity."

"I'll… tell," Kurt gritted out, though Shane didn't appear to hear. At the end of the corridor, in the noisy chaos of A&E, a woman was singing in an unfamiliar language. A folk song, mournful and high.

Shane drew a finger along Kurt's chin, wiping away the spittle. "He tastes good, doesn't he? Like cherries."

Kurt had to throw up. He wanted to, but couldn't. His insides weighed too much, a bag of sharp rocks. Shane's smile blurred in and out, too large and too close. Kurt tried to cover his eyes, but his hands wouldn't cooperate.

"He inspires protective feelings," Shane was saying. "I understand. You're a decent man, Kurt, and I like you. My own tutors used to thrash me 'til I bled. Different attitude then. But you must understand, Joshua does not belong to you. He is ours."

I will tell

Shane helped Kurt into a chair. His spine had lost its solidity, so Shane draped his arm around his shoulders, keeping him up, as if to comfort him. The touch sent a hot shock down Kurt's spine. His trousers were wet. His socks.

"One drop at a time, Kurt, in the beginning. Terribly important, as we learnt with the Corsican children."

I will put a

Put a stop

A nurse came out and asked Shane if he was family. Shane stood, tall and strong and young, coursing with sunlit vitality, thrumming in Kurt's vision like a faulty florescent light.

A stop to

This

|The Fireman|

~

The Anvil has been anchored off Majorca for a week and a day. None may go ashore and none may board us.

It is not a physician's place to speak charitably of superstition. I break this personal imperative only to log my interactions with a patient of mine, one Mister Sheppard, a stoker aboard this vessel.

The dissection of the unexplained, I believe, is the scientist's anchor. Like inclement weather, the inexplicable may take many forms, and what may begin as a spatter of rain is liable to become a typhoon in an instant. In climates such as these we must hold fast, with all the cool-headed dignity we can muster.

Nevertheless, I am resolved to burn these pages.

Able Seaman Sheppard. 32 years of age. A Norfolk man, and a lifelong sailor. A glance at his records shows the complaints one would expect from a man who shovels coal all day: minor burns and lacerations, one amputated toe. Nothing to suggest an unsound mind.

Sheppard first came to the infirmary on the morning of the eighteenth of July, 1883. We had left Portsmouth some eight weeks prior, touring the usual spots, with no action. An ironclad vessel has no need to show its strength. The mere presence of the Anvil scatters all foes to the wind. That morning, we were cruising along the coast of Portugal, allowing the sails to do most of the work.

My young assistant, Mister Harris, ushered Sheppard in with the customary crustiness which endears him to no one but me. Sheppard loitered, eyeing the cabinets of bottles with their impenetrable Latin labels. Harris knew the man in passing. He was a sociable fellow, Harris told me, known amongst the men as something of a humourist, and I took his reticence to mean he had some embarrassing ailment of the nether regions. I was about to reassure him, as I did all the men, that

I spend my life examining the private parts of sailors and find them quite tedious, but something in Sheppard's face stayed my tongue.

The stokers are envied and pitied in equal measure. These men are paid more than regular seaman, another half in fact, and are provided with baths and good soap for when they come off watch. But the poor souls work in Hell. I have seen these men cough up chunks of foaming black matter and take no notice. Eight hundred and fifty tonnes of coal won't be mastered without a fight, but they must do so, in white uniforms.

To my surprise, Sheppard required a sleeping draught.

Though it is unusual for a stoker to struggle to rest, even surrounded by his snoring crewmates, it is not unheard of. I furnished Sheppard with a mild opiate and instructed him to take three drops in water before settling into his hammock. He thanked me, nodded to Harris, who ignored him, and returned to the engine room.

The Anvil was somewhere off Lisbon, I believe, when Sheppard returned. He was sour with perspiration, as was I. We were caught in an unusually hot pocket of weather. The wind had fallen and engines were on full steam. Harris was more short-tempered than usual, to my personal amusement.

"If you still can't sleep, don't consider yourself part of a select club," Harris said.

The stoker stood in the infirmary doorway, cap in hand. He looked haggard – indeed more nervous than before, as if this time I might prescribe the knife. "Begging your pardon, sir. It's been days."

"Very well. Let's take a look at you. Are you in pain?"

As I waved him over, Sheppard was muscled out of the way by a young sailor in a state of agitation. "Sir! Sir, someone's come a cropper."

Harris was up and handing me my bag before the man could finish his sentence.

It was Harold Walsh, one of our young rawbones. I drew up the death certificate: born 1864, died 1883. It appears he fell afoul of the steep ladder leading down to the engine room. A superficial autopsy revealed no obvious alcohol consumption. Sweaty palms slipping on the handrails, I imagine. No one saw him fall. If he did not die instantly, I wrote in the log, he did so wretchedly alone.

The Anvil chugged on unchallenged. The officers spoke of boredom and passed the time by handing out floggings to any man without pristine uniform. I thought with sympathy of the stokers, heaving and sweating down in the engine room in their stiff white cotton. I had forgotten Sheppard entirely.

August brought further misfortune. One afternoon, Harris and I were preparing to treat a lad with a broken femur, so I confess I took little notice of Sheppard's demeanour when he interrupted us. Nevertheless, he would not leave until I gave him another sleeping draught.

The break was a bad one. We had no choice but to amputate.

"It's alright, McDowell. We have chloroform," I told him, smiling so the lad would think I hadn't seen the tears in his eyes. "And you aren't my first."

Harris made a face as we washed our hands. "Someone ought to do something about those ladders. He must have gone down like a cannonball to snap a bone like that."

Out of McDowell's sight, Harris opened the case of saws and forceps. He offered me a tight smile. He knew I hated the business of butchery, and I was grateful for his concern.

"Ash on my kit," McDowell snivelled as Harris held him down. "They'll hang me."

"Even our captain wouldn't hang a man for a smut on a sleeve," Harris said, smoothing McDowell's hair from his eyes.

But McDowell was delirious with pain. "Everyone—will—know."

I covered the patient's nose and mouth with the ether mask, and set my mind to my grisly task.

At a quarter past two, I was awoken. Despite bathing, I reeked of another man's blood, and a hot wave of it turned my stomach. Someone was banging on the cabin door. Harris swore as he slithered out of bed. He didn't bother to don shoes or jacket.

Sheppard, wheezing like a locomotive, had been dragged to the infirmary by a pair of sailors. He was keeping them awake, they said. There was something wrong with him.

I peeled back the stoker's eyelids to see blood vessels like a map of the tides. "Is he drunk?"

"We tried that, sir. Nothing calms him. Look."

The sailor snatched up Sheppard's calloused hand. The thumbnail was prised from its bed like an oyster shell.

"He's using splinters from the deck. Shoving them up there, the great pillock."

"Sheppard? Will you speak to me?"

But the stoker was staring over my shoulder, at the aprons we'd hung up to dry after working on McDowell. I had thought them clean, but in the lamplight they were rusty and stiff with blood. Sheppard gave a low wail. When the other sailors tightened their grip, he lashed out.

"McDowell's his mate," said one man. "Not taking his death well."

Harris yawned. "He isn't dead. A little lighter, but he'll keep."

I judged it the sensible thing to say. I was mistaken.

It took both sailors, Harris and myself to prevent Sheppard from dashing out his brains against the wall.

I was panting as we pinned his flailing limbs to the deck. "Sheppard, I don't want to restrain you, but you leave me little choice."

"Everyone will know." He wasn't talking to me. He stared up at our swinging aprons with shining eyes.

"Know what?" I said.

I was glad of Harris at my side as we strapped him into bed.

A more stifling night I could not imagine. I dreamt of fire, of the Hell below me in the engine room. Men in ashen uniforms peeling them away along with their skin, hanging them up to dry like the aprons in the infirmary.

I can generally rely on Harris to wake me with coffee and a modicum of gruff sympathy. That morning, though, he was otherwise engaged.

Through the cabin wall I heard him holler my name – wreathed in blasphemy – and I sprang up, stumbling half-dressed into the infirmary.

Even now I can scarcely believe what I saw. As Harris raised the alarm, I checked the supply cabinets. Locked, just as I left them. All surgical implements were accounted for. McDowell's sickbed was rumpled, but empty. Our patient was gone.

I shook Sheppard, sprawled in the adjacent bunk. "Did you see him go?"

He rubbed at his eyes with sooty knuckles. "I slept," he said, and with alarm, I realised his restraints were unbuckled.

"Mister Harris," he explained. "In the night. Said he hated seeing a man strung up like a bit of gammon."

I paced the room. It made no sense. New amputees don't hoist themselves up and go for a stroll. For one thing, I had left McDowell no crutches. We had given Sheppard enough opium to fell an elephant; even if he had seen something, he would never remember it.

Need I say the search for McDowell was futile? Harris and I were not at liberty to join the hunt. Three men were admitted with sickness and diarrhoea, which is no laughing matter in an enclosed space. My day was spent administering fluids and dodging spillages, cursing the heat and the stench with every breath. Harris was all too pleased to shoo Sheppard back to work with a few choice words about malingering. The stoker was pale, but satisfactorily improved, I thought, for the rest.

Harris and I took our supper on deck that night, looking out at the sultry lights of Cadiz. In all our years working within inches of one another, I had come to know his ways in microscopic detail, and he mine. There is power in intimate companionship. Our communication, like that of twins, was largely silent.

I was not surprised when, after cajoling me into forcing down some buttered bread, Harris spoke of McDowell. "Could he have pitched himself overboard?"

"It's possible. The loss of a limb can drive men to it."

There was no need to voice my thoughts about the ladders he would have to climb, drained and dressed as he was, like a lamb in a butcher's window. Neither was I prepared to speak of my feelings, half-formed and slippery in the muggy night air. But Harris knew. Our thoughts are made of similar tissue.

"I've displeased you."

"No," I said, glad to stop short of *never*. "You are indispensable. I only… I must know I can depend on you. Setting Sheppard loose like that. You ought to have asked."

Harris's face screwed into an amused grimace. "The man was delirious. I wouldn't set him loose any more than I'd let a bull run about the place. You're cracked, old man. You haven't had a decent night's sleep in weeks. You'll have untied him and forgotten." He looked into his tea, swirled it around in the cup. The distant city of Cadiz reflected in his eyes, an uneasy glimmer. "Just… watch yourself."

"Whatever do you mean?"

Harris patted my arm. "I'll fetch us something stronger."

The heat of Cadiz was more hateful than that of Portugal. I was tempted to take one of my own sleeping draughts. I dreamt of the blue spectre of cholera, of decks awash with blood and effluvia. They took me to the engine room, those dreams, a roiling pit of smoke. Stokers crept about like damned souls hoping not to be singled out by the Devil's knowing eyes. The utter nakedness of the dissecting table. All secrets revealed. I thrashed in my bunk, searching for the exit. I wasn't a stoker. I wasn't like them. I hadn't *done* anything.

I woke with a yell when Harris threw a pillow at me.

No cholera, thank God. My patients had consumed some bad salt beef. The Anvil powered on around the south of Spain, unchallenged, alone.

When I heard the tentative knock, I did not have to look up from my ledgers.

"Come in, Sheppard. How are the fingernails?"

"You been expecting me, sir?"

"I am a doctor, Sheppard. I have seen every fleshly horror you can imagine…" I spoke as gently as I could. Still, his shoulders stiffened. I went on: "…but few things rattle me like a man on the brink of addiction."

"Sir?"

"First begging for a sleeping draught, then these strange commotions. You've been fighting it, but you need it now, don't you?"

His hair was lank with sweat. Curiously, when he shook his head, I could see he meant it.

I bade him sit, taking note of his trembling hands. A sure sign of dependence. "You knew McDowell, didn't you? You were mates."

He scratched at a smear of pale ash on his cheek. "You got that secrecy, haven't you? You doctors. Like priests."

I assured him confidentiality was my watchword.

He pondered this for some time. "I liked McDowell," he said quietly. "He was a good sort."

"And Walsh?"

"He had a… an agreeable singing voice." Sheppard's damp throat worked through a swallow. "I liked his songs."

"One friend dead. And another, most likely. You're grieving, man. It will pass. But the second you turn to opium, or to drink…"

I must have said something foolish. Sheppard interrupted me, unexpectedly intense: "You ever been in down the engine room?"

"I admit, I take care not to."

"I've been a stoker since I were fifteen. Hard work. But good. Work like that don't give you time for brewing things over. You got your work and you got your mates and that's your lot. You follow me?"

I did, in my own way. But Sheppard's force alarmed me.

"I was all alright 'til I saw him sitting there."

At this, my eyes flicked up. "Sitting? On duty?"

The stoker gave an unpleasant laugh. "He has his own idea of duty, sir."

"Look here, Sheppard, you don't have to give me a name, but there are strict protocols for a reason. Someone could die."

He rubbed his dirty cheek. I fancied the ash sat beneath the dermis somehow, like the tattooed sailors of Singapore Harris spoke of in tones of awe.

"Sheppard, tell me. Did McDowell neglect his duty? Or Walsh?"

"He isn't one of us."

"You're not making sense, man."

"He sits *inside* the furnace."

Sheppard as good as bellowed it at me.

On examination, his eyes were bloodshot but responsive to light, his pulse thready but nothing to be concerned about. I palpated his liver: no enlargement. No immediate sign of venereal disease. He was hot, but weren't we all?

"We all see things in the flames," he said, having wrestled back his composure. "Down there in the dark all day, you see all sorts dancing about. Usually it's horses, for me, galloping and gone. A lot see faces, but—" Sheppard met my eyes and held them fast. "There was a man. Sitting. Inside the furnace."

"Was?" I contained my scepticism. A nervous invalid must be met with compassion, not scorn. "He's gone now?"

"It's worse when he's gone."

"Describe him to me."

"You know what a man looks like, sir."

"A man impervious to flame." Perhaps repeating it would bring him to his senses. But I suspected Sheppard was beyond the reach of logic.

"He watches me," he said. "When I feed the boiler. He's there when I come on duty and stays right through till the end of my shift. He don't bother no one else."

"And why is that?"

"I can't say."

"You don't know?"

"I cannot *say*."

He feared this man. I did not insult him by acknowledging it.

"You said it's worse when he isn't in the flames. Why is that?"

"He goes a'wandering. He comes up to the gundeck now, when we're sleeping. I see his footprints in ash, all around the hammocks. He likes the ones who talk. In their sleep, like." He stiffened at a noise; only Harris bumping around in our cabin next door. "McDowell was a talker."

"And you want sleep. Sleep so deep you don't know if this phantom is there or not."

"I did want that. But now he gets inside. I'll be dreaming of my mother and my sister at the dinner table in Cromer, and I'll be passing the beer jug to Mary and then he's sitting there, smouldering like a side of roast mutton." Sheppard placed his head in his hands. "And then he opens his mouth…"

I do not relish the sight of a crying man. I recommended Sheppard be placed on light duties until his condition improved. No sense having a nervous sailor in the engine room. As I said, someone could die.

In the week following this disquieting exchange, more men complained of cramps and fever. I administered purgatives, fasting them until the invading force was starved out. I kept a close eye on Harris in case the contagion should touch him. Sheppard was right about one thing; you have your work and you have your mates, and that is enough.

The Anvil was buffeted like a toy in a tin bath as the heat converged into thick cloud and a spiteful wind.

When one is on duty, a storm is the enemy to be fought and overcome. But to lie there and helplessly endure is a torment for any sailor. Doubled up on his bunk, one of my patients – a softly-spoken young steward – trembled head to toe. I went to him without thinking, knelt down, and gave his hand a heartening squeeze.

The ship moaned as a hard wave caught us portside. There came a wheezing laugh behind us. My patient jerked his hand away and I turned, surprised at Harris for the edge of cruelty in his tone. But Harris was away, fetching clean water.

I could at least make myself presentable for his return. My uniform was disgracefully spattered. One privilege of my position is that no officer will flog me for disorderly kit. Unlike poor McDowell, so terrified of a few spots of ash he made them his last words.

It disturbed me, Sheppard's story. That whole week, it had haunted me. Not for the outlandish content, but his conviction. Sheppard was afraid – so afraid that manly bluster was eclipsed entirely. I was accustomed to such unpleasantness in the operating theatre: a physiological reaction to a physical threat. But what was the root of Sheppard's terror? The spark that created this 'fireman' of his?

I tried to picture such a man. A ghoul who laughs and threatens to – what? In Sheppard's dreams, he invades a quiet Cromer parlour and opens his mouth. To bite, I wondered? Or to curse?

It were as if I had called for him. In the infirmary doorway, Sheppard had a jug of steaming water and a weary smile on his face. I experienced a queer feeling, as if someone had shone a light on my innermost thoughts. In a trice, I was sickened, outraged – and, I realised, prickling with fear. As Sheppard stood there, brazenly scrutinising me with bloodshot eyes, I considered how easy it would be to snatch up any one of my surgical implements and extinguish him like a lamp.

What a fool I had been.

"Where is Harris?" I demanded.

A smear of ash marred the stoker's slackened mouth.

He would not tell.

With an oath, I was on my feet. I broke my duty of care to the men lying around me. Sheppard made no attempt to stop me leaving. I moved as if through a dream, down ladders, slipping and bumping with the fevered motion of the waves. I passed the spot where Walsh met his end, where McDowell – talkative McDowell – had failed to die when Sheppard first pushed him.

No preternatural creature could compel a man to murder. I made this my litany as I raced to the engine room. Sails were up. Even deep in the bowels of the ship, I could hear them clinking urgently above the relentless churning of the boilers. At the engine room hatch I faltered, seized by the heat emanating from within. I should have brought a pistol. I was too soft for this, whatever it was. I ought to return to my post, to wait for Harris with a plate of buttered bread and some hot tea to toast his return. Oh, but how then to live with myself? With my hands on the iron wheel, I set my teeth against the burn, my eyes shut tight against whatever lay inside.

I could call his name, yet I could not.

Everyone would know.

|The Frost of Heaven|

The bitterest winter on record, the man on the wireless said. Still, I rather like it. The Fens, they used to say, was good for three things: malaria, incest, and insanity. Living here requires tenacity. I like to think of it as proof of my renewed dedication to holiness.

You came to me for a glimpse of that, I take it. The spectacle of the modern hermit.

I imagine you'd rather have done so in the spring, though. You can keep your gloves on, I don't mind. I see you are serious. Pacing won't warm you up, I can tell you that. I've done pacing enough for both of us these past forty years. You can't imagine forty years, can you? You are — what? Twenty? Too young to be forced into such a decision. That was what they demanded of you, was it not? To decide.

What long hair you have. I take it you've been away from the seminary for quite some time. Look at those curls. Is that the fashion, nowadays? Ringlets, practically.

Twenty. In my experience, it galls them. The sight of youth. They remember theirs, the decisions they made. Back then, a man chose his profession before he was breeched and he stuck with it. I've always admired young lads willing to brave the wilderness.

Have a brandy. Don't be coy. I shan't, if you don't mind. My work requires a steady hand.

Youth is for trying everything. Liking all of it, or none of it, and wanting more, or less, or whichever is hardest to attain. Saint Francis was a wild young man. He frittered away his boyhood on drink and girls and bad friends. Spent his father's money on *sensation*. Francis was always something of a preoccupation of mine.

I must admit, I am impressed you found me. I don't suppose anyone has breathed my name in Cambridge since the old king died. They painted over the murals right away. One of my little acolytes sent me a letter. Black-edged envelope. Apparently, my work verged on heresy. Certainly passed the boundaries of good taste.

It was a crime back then, see. So much more so than now.

Visionary? Merely nudes. But I was careless in my personal affairs. A little talent and a little fame can be ruinous to a weak character, and I was tolerated until I started leading the young ones astray. They tried to keep the papers oblivious, but inevitably…

Well. It's no good to dwell.

I fled to Gibraltar. Europa Point – the farthest one can go before toppling into the sea. Can't say I wasn't tempted.

Yes, warm there! And the churches are different. Life-size wax saints. The most curious thing. Wearing clothes like you and I, with beautiful painted eyes and red lips and real hair. I made a habit of visiting one particular church near my lodgings to escape the midday heat, and sketch a little. Every day, I'd sit there, looked upon by Joseph of Arimathea and the whole crew. Francis was there, arms out, like this, holding wax doves with real feathers. The *look* they'd managed to capture on his face. Gave me a pleasant sort of chill, being alone with him, as if I were being touched somehow, by something old and understanding. And when I met his glass eyes… Well, it's one thing to offer up one's sins to a priest. But these figures…

I dared to touch him, once. His skin was dry and just a little pliant. And cold.

Eerie? I suppose. I grew to rather love them. Nothing here is quite so— Pardon?

Fleshly.

That is the very word.

I missed English winters, in the end. Call it penitence. So I slunk home, or as close to home as I dared. Bought this cottage. The wind screams in from every direction. No trees to hold it back. No hills, certainly no journalists. They call Yorkshire God's country, but in the Fens there's nowhere to hide from His eyes. It gets a man to thinking, out here on his own.

No, don't lean forward. I've no wisdom to impart.

My studio? Through there. I still work. Though my medium has changed, somewhat.

Looking for models? Dear boy, I can see why you came to blows at the seminary. They don't take kindly to young men aware of their own gravity. You've a good face, though. I can almost see you in one of my old murals.

My work has changed since then. I am improving myself.

You remind me of Francis. You do. Comely and dark. His was a wild youth. But he grew tired of drinking dens and trysts – *sensation*. He questioned, as you have. His friends mocked him for his newfound piety, and his father was furious. Francis was made for better things, he said; for business, for filling the family coffers. Francis took himself off to a cave to think on his future. For a man accustomed to pleasure and comfort, the cold stone was a shock to his very soul. One night, wandering the freezing woodland, Francis was set upon by bandits who beat him and stole his clothes. Francis was left naked and shivering – more alone and helpless than he had ever been. And yet *transformed*. By losing everything – every comfort, every friend, every thread of attachment to the world that once welcomed him so warmly – Francis became the holy man we venerate today. It gave him strength, that night of hardship. A second chance.

You prefer the tale of his stigmata? Well, the young do thirst for blood, I suppose. Francis himself craved war and glory, before his transformation in that cold countryside.

Have another brandy.

You've been given your marching orders, then. Either pop on a dog collar and brace yourself for a life of village fêtes, or go out into the world and let it taint you. Well, who better to help you decide than an old man who has most decidedly taken both paths? You've told no one of your coming here, I take it?

The daylight fades quickly here. Out on the marshes, you'll see ghost lights flare up in the dusk. Will-o'-the-wisps. Pretty, but they tempt you out, into danger. It's a pagan thing, this landscape. The cold creeps in. I forgo a fire for as long as I can bear. I worry that by seeking out comfort, I will… fall short again.

You feel the same. I'm glad.

I imagine my old colleagues prefer to think of me as dead. I have visitors so infrequently. Around the first real cold snap, usually, and always you lone seminary boys who've heard a ghastly story in the dormitories. No, I'm glad of the notoriety. Without it I would never have had the chance to get to know those boys so intimately. And I am grateful to them. Come back and paint, they say. No one likes a martyr. But they're wisps, those boys. Tempters. What I want is so much harder to attain. Francis would understand. You do. You aren't yet tainted, as I was at your age. I can feel it.

Oh.

You've nodded off.

Forgive the rush. It's just that we've already lost much of the light.

Goodness me, what a lot of clothes you've piled on. Lie still, if you don't mind. I shall have to slit them open.

Into the studio with you, there's a lamb.

Bracing, isn't it? This section of the roof caved in about a decade ago. Heavy snowfall. Turned out to be ideal. One feels the benefit of the dramatic spotlight when everything's set up.

Oh, never mind him. He turned out not to be the one. I should have known it when he drove up here in that low-slung snarling car of his. No one driving a beast like that would ever be in danger of sainthood. He was very much the pre-transformation Francis, like the others before him. Seeking me out for morbid amusement. Not like you, with your searching mind. Anyway, the car's in the marsh, and so will he be, soon. No good dwelling on mistakes.

Let's rig you up before things get challenging. You're roughly the same height as our disappointing friend over there. Saves me the trouble of adjusting the stand. First the left arm… and the right. I can see why you admire the Franciscan stigmata; you have beautiful wrists. And these ringlets. Think of all the birds who'll nestle in them.

During the months of transformation, it has always been my hope that a darling little muntjac deer will wander in and curl up at your bare feet. What a sight that would be.

Now, I like to start with a liberal rubbing of borax. The frost will help kill some of the germs, obviously, but you never can be too careful. Then a nice coating of boiled arsenic soap to prime the canvas. I prefer to build up the flesh tones gently, else we end up with a rather opaque look, most unsatisfactory. And then, when you are perfect and pristine, the final veneer of wax. Don't worry; I've perfected my technique. I've had a good while to practise. And I have clothes for you, also. Brown

Franciscan cowls, a great many of them, which I will wash and change as need dictates.

The rest is up to you.

When this long winter comes to an end – when the ground is thawing and the shoots begin to peek between your toes, and I can at last sleep without the bite of this merciless wind – I will enter this room one morning to find you smiling at me. Radiant with the holiness of one who has come through the cold and been *remade*.

And you will take me with you.

|The Forlorn Hope|

~

Vultures wheeled above the walled city of Perdu, their shrieks carried off by another surge of harried bells. In the fossilised desert below, an army tended to its rations and other essential business.

"On this day, the 12th of June 1813, I, Captain Matilda Cross, being sound in mind, make these directions to be carried out in the event of my death. I make this final Will in the presence of two witnesses, Sergeant Garrick and Private Welby of the 45th Infantry. In this, my thirty-sixth year—"

At the camp's heart, the girls were boiling beef and singing.

Billywitch, Billywitch,
Fly away home,
Your house is on fire,
Your children will burn.

"—and so many miles from my place of birth, I trust unto my executors – is that what you call them, kid? – to carry out my wishes to the letter."

Welby was a nice little thing, if a touch bovine. A failed scholar, she had a fair hand and didn't pull any faces. Garrick, as expected, had done nothing but gripe since Cross had called her to the tent.

"Ma'am…"

Captain Cross scraped back her hair and treated the Irishwoman to one of her stares. "To my sergeant Rose Garrick I leave my rifle, on account of it being better than hers at almost everything, chiefly hitting Frenchies. My boots… I don't know. Whoever they fit. My sword I leave to Lady Amelia Fitzmichael of Whitewater House, Surrey, in gratitude for her teaching me letters back in ninety-five. She always did like a trophy above the fireplace."

Garrick made the throaty sound that usually meant the latrines were ripe in the midday sun. To her, Lady Fitzmichael was *That Woman*. But the sergeant had at least made tea. She was as good at brewing tea as she was at killing, which was slapdash but fast, and precisely when Cross needed it. "Beg pardon, Ma'am," she said, passing Cross a tin mug. "But I expect the good lady will prefer you alive."

"The good lady has forty acres and a strapping husband worth five hundred a year. She can't have everything she wants."

My own dear Mathilde,

What is this I hear of you burning my letters? Have you forgotten my million eyes? Or is this silence your crude method of wounding me? Alley cat. Only ever come running when I turn my back…

"'S just as I see it, Ma'am." The sergeant slapped a mosquito on her swarthy forearm.

A fresh clamour of bells rang out over Perdu. Welby jolted, sending a fine spray of ink across the document. That morning, artillery had made a mountain of the city wall. They were all still chewing on the dust. With a telescope, Cross saw the mess the Billywitches had made of the golden city since they took it in the spring. Bright pennants hung in ribbons. Temple domes reduced to eggshells. Of the citizens she saw no sign, but she knew the 'Witches were in there, the way she knew a scorpion was in her boot without needing to tip it up first. Every city, it was always the same. How they got in, no one was sure. Pagan excess, the Army chaplains said; tainted meat, said the surgeons. A half-dead priest they found in Shallamar spoke of old things, things that chase, but he was mad with fever and would have said anything for a drop of water.

When Cross used the handful of local words she knew to question the nomad shepherd boys, they clicked their tongues and rode away. Welby was the linguist, but when Cross sent her out to speak to them, she came back pink with embarrassment and apologies.

"Come on, then," Cross demanded. "What did the little buggers say?"

Only that they were wary of the woman with the yellow hair and the black look.

My own dear Mathilde,

Silence still? Sleepless, I unlocked the chest in the attic and spent the night barefoot amongst your dazzling old letters.

Despite this and all the rest, I still show my face at church on Sundays. Picture me beneath my widest bonnet with the veil of lace – what did you used to call it? My mosquito helmet. I sit there in the family pew and listen to the neighbours trotting out the usual topics. Births, marriages, and you, *my dear. Everyone reads of your daring deeds. Mister Dalrymple boasts it was he who first gave you the notion of taking the King's shilling. Wasn't he the one you oh-so-carelessly pricked with a toasting fork when he made that snide remark about dirty petticoats? He says he saw potential in you, the way one sees it in a man. I think about that fork daily.*

Missus Dixon is just as bad. She and her hideous coterie all claim they remember you here, that they shared some special little interaction with you when you were nothing but my maid, though we both know that's a lie and a poor one at that. The motherless waif, Matilda Cross. That particular untruth was your own, was it not?

I miss your barefaced lies, Mathilde. I miss your promises, sweet as your threats. You will come home to me this instant. You will.

The volunteers of the Forlorn Hope would go up at daybreak. The first over the rubble. The first to see the whites, the yellows, the reds of their eyes. Captain Cross's name was dry on the roster before anyone else had the chance to sign.

"The girls are welcome to raise a glass in my name if they see fit," she said. "Sergeant Garrick can have any last pennies to my name, what good they'll do her. As for my body…"

"Ma'am?" Welby looked up from the page. Brown eyes, unplucked brows. She was a decent soldier, but looking at Welby, Cross found her brain crowded with cannonballs and agues and festering wounds, and she resented the private for flaunting her fragility, for passing on that burden.

"My body is not to be repatriated."

Garrick flashed her teeth. "What about Sophia?"

"She took a vow of poverty. She has no need of any baubles from me."

"She'll want to bury her mother, Ma'am."

The bells rang out. Rose Garrick's broad handsome face was the same grim mask Cross first lay eyes on in the column that scorching summer in Spain when the enemy was merely Napoleon. Cross missed Boney. That was soldiering, not this grinding routine of ruins and rumours. When the word came down from Horse Guards that the Billywitches were Boney's secret weapon, Cross slung her sword over her shoulder and strolled down the line. Any day now, she promised the girls, they would capture one of the bastards, cut it open and make sense of it, just like any other bit of kit. When it became apparent Boney was fighting the 'Witches too, Cross found she had no words of reassurance.

It was around then that the letters started again.

That flawless arcane script. Waiting for her on the camp bed. At once she was undone, staring down at the brown ink Amelia favoured, bloody and costly, like all her favourite things. Cross had taken those memories and killed them, or so she believed, but now they were crowding the tent with her, threatening to whip away the canvas and expose her to the whole battalion.

Sophia's name brought that unsteady feeling back. She recalled her grown daughter in the roughspun habit of a nun, that dust cloud of hair, so like her own, pinned and covered until she could be anyone's daughter, or no one's. The only thing that linked them that final day as the elders sang in the bell tower was a shared love of uniform. "*When your grandmother was young...*" she almost said. But an officer never lowered her guard, especially not an officer baptised in the oily effluvia of the Birmingham Inkleys.

And what would speaking accomplish? *When your grandmother was young, she fastened my dress to hers with a length of twine. She told me the neighbours pressed their faces to the mouseholes and took note of our comings and goings. That if she let me out of her sight for even a second, they would spring from their hiding places to snatch me away and she would die, die, die, Matilda, do you want that? They're ringing my death knell across the parish, listen...*

Captain Cross left Sophia in the Sacred Heart where the water came clean from the mountains and the bells only marked the passing of hours.

My own dear Mathilde, alley cat, wretch…

There's no problem you cannot take a blade to, is there? Always something to prove. When I found you, you were everything they say about the tenements. The perfume of the slaughterhouse. I had to burn your clothes to kill the lice, and no matter how hard we scrubbed your filthy skin or how prettily I taught you to simper and bob in the presence of your betters, you were a corroded thing, eaten up with the need to bite and scratch and claw your way out of the Rag Castle streets, and when you saw you could not win this coward's battle, you turned tail and scurried off the way your kind are born to.

Damn you, Matilda. I've been sitting here debating whether or not to destroy this page, and now my coffee is cold. You always did delight in wasting my time.

There's a splinter in me. Always has been. Perhaps that mutual savagery is what drew us to one another. You read my letters and curse me for my cruelty and my pride? Of course you do. Each note I send to you, I send loathing myself. Do you ever recollect those long evenings together, with J at his club and the house empty? The two of us, free! To talk and to dream. With my money and your bravery, we had the means for every adventure under the sun. How privileged we were, in our secretive way. And now you are so far away, and I am split in two.

I won't let you make a fool of me, speaking to thin air like this. Be a good girl and write. I have something for you.

Garrick grimaced at the gritty film on her tea. "It's a damn fool thing you're doing, Ma'am, and I don't mind you knowing it."

"I've been promised certain death in a hundred places. But *this*. This is certain promotion."

"You're in one of your moods."

Cross could feel Welby holding her breath. The little private spent the four months at sea hugging a bucket. Cross, unfazed by the relentless swell and plunge, intended to use the time to question the Indian Sepoys about their destination. But they knew only as much as she did, missionaries' tales of beastly red fruits wet on the outside, spiked toads you could lick to lose a memory, shifting sands the colour of a week-old bruise. To her relief, all wonderfully true. This disconcerting island everyone despised was migraine bright, too addictively treacherous to allow space in the mind for anything or anyone else. Cross knew people like that. You could disappear inside them if you didn't keep reminding yourself of your own dwindling solidity like some fanatical faith.

Four months of salt water between her and Birmingham. A year in the desert.

Everyone else spent their last days of home leave full of gin, scrawling their names and kill tallies on the inn walls, but not Captain Cross. She boarded the dawn coach to The Inkleys with a knife in her boot and her money sewn into the lining of her greatcoat.

"They pulled the tenements down, miss," the barmaid said, sopping up spilled ale with a rag as grey as the hollows under her eyes. "A good ten years past. Well overdue, if you ask me. Forgive me, but I don't remember any Harriet, miss. We see a lot of people come and go."

But Cross wasn't thinking about that now.

"Welby, cover your ears," Garrick said.

She blinked owlishly. "Sergeant?"

"Think loud thoughts, you silly chit. Matilda, remember Dundril. You were doing well there. Sleeping. Eating. This shithole was known for its doctors. I got talking to the nomads—"

So the secretive swine would happily speak to Cross's sergeant. A plume of smoke feathered out above the battlements. A bad colour, to Cross's eye. And those unceasing bastard bells. Welby – with her inky hands over her ears, why had Garrick made her do that? – was staring out at the ruined defences as if the Billywitches might come pouring down in an avalanche while they slept. It knocked the wind out of you, the first time. Private Welby hadn't had many first times.

Cross felt Garrick watching her. She was always watching her, it was her job, and Cross had come to rely on those following eyes, hard mirrors in which to gauge her decisions. But now there was something unfamiliar there, and it was making Cross' sword hand itch.

"I hate to ask, Ma'am," said Garrick. "And you can tell me to button my lip. But what has that woman—"

"Nothing."

My own dear Mathilde,

A drizzly afternoon here in Surrey. A day for shawls and novels, and, for the lucky ones, the company of a friend. When did you last see drizzle?

I'd wager you miss it on some animal level, your dismal habitat. Has your skin bronzed in all this time away? I worried about that, you know, seeing you trussed up in that red tunic for the first time. Life is cheap but good skin is a luxury few can afford.

Since my last letter the fruits in the Whitewater gardens have ripened and fulfilled their destiny as jam. Fashions, too, are changing. Missus Dixon and her friends are cavorting around in gowns embellished with gold frogging and slippers of finest faux Billywitch leather, their mode of supporting our heroic soldiers overseas. I attach a sketch for your amusement.

Time is passing, dear Mathilde, and still you have not written to me. I could take this to mean you are dead. If that were so, I could wear darkest crepe and collect my tears in a bottle like all the other decorative widows. But my million eyes know better.

Do you ever look about you at your comrades and wonder who among them is doing my work, watching over you? It could be anyone. That hulking Irish woman, the one who hates me? That would be a comic turn. You trust her. Remember when you trusted me?

My million eyes watched you all those months ago when you took the dawn coach to Birmingham. You once told me no one ventured into the Inkleys from the outside. All too easy to slip inside and dissolve into the shadows. No, no one takes that coach alone, not unless they are looking for something. Fights and flesh, you always said.

What about family?

Cross saw the sting on Garrick's face. With care, she tried again. "Rose, I've no special inclination to die tomorrow. But if it pleases you, find the 'Witch that kills me and take its head. Boil it up and send the skull to Sophia's convent. You can do all of that before you ever march me to any poxy physician. But I mean it – you do not put my bones in a box and send them back to England."

Garrick chewed on nothing. "So I'm up there picking through the rubble and see you lying there and I do what?"

"You keep going."

Garrick tossed her tea away in disgust. It sank into the sand leaving hardly a trace. "A fine sergeant I am."

The tent was thick with baleful silence. The night was rolling in, bringing with it that uncanny rush of cold the women had come to crave, peeling off their woollen tunics to let their aching hides breathe. Still the vultures made their grim circuit over Perdu. Little Welby saw Cross neglecting her tea to watch them.

"They kill plague," Welby said. "The miasma will survive the death of the host and jump to the nearest warm body, but a vulture can put an end to it by eating the infected flesh. Like a living furnace." The private spoke with a zest for information that made her easy to tease, but now no one was laughing she looked unsure. As she trailed off, she picked bashfully at her inky nails. "It's… quite beautiful, really."

Garrick met Cross's notorious stare with one of her own.

"Cowbag," the sergeant muttered.

The things I do for you, my Mathilde. The places I go. The things I discover.

Dear old Harriet. She knits beautifully, you never told me. Despite her arthritis, she stitches away like a busy little squirrel, and when you compliment her handiwork she grunts churlishly. You really are terribly alike.

My dear, your mother will live out her days in perfect comfort. I found her – for you. You needn't know where or in what circumstances, for I know they will cause you pain. No chains for her, no public viewings. I bought her a private room at Rubery Hill. Good food, country air, the companionship of a sweet, strict nurse. As far as she knows, kind-hearted benefactresses keep old widows out of the madhouse all the time. What a nice world she inhabits, up there in her head.

It doesn't all have to be degradation, Matilda.

You will come home when your posting is over, and I will take you to her. And then, when you have dispensed with this pig-headed obstinance of yours, you will allow my physicians to examine you for traces of Harriet's splinters. Modern ideas. You will be well, and we will be happy. I would hate to disturb Sophia at her convent, but you will agree it is only right a member of the family is involved in Harriet's care. Sophia hasn't met her grandmother, has she?

Picture a million eyes, Mathilde, every one of them brimming with love.

"For I know my Redeemer liveth, et cetera," said Cross. "It's done?"

Welby blew gently on the ink. "All but the signatures, Ma'am."

They both looked to Garrick. She took the opportunity to pack her pipe with tobacco, licking the crumbs from her fingers where they clung to the callouses ground deep by years on the road.

"She's poison is what she is, Ma'am."

Captain Cross turned her face away to the walled city of Perdu, little more than a noisy inkblot against the darkening sky. Here night mugged you, it sneaked up behind on silent feet and clamped a hand over your mouth. The vultures took their leave with the daylight, though where they bedded down in this barren land, she couldn't guess.

|Grim|

~

I rise from my den at first dark. The sun sets early in late October, the relics of it cooling under my claws as I commence the Prowl.

It is mine, the Prowl, a liturgy learned by rote. Whether the grass is summer-crisp or at peace under a layer of snow, I make my nightly circuit over tumbled flint and ivy-choked stone.

I greet the Dead with a nudge of my hoary snout. At rest. At rest. At rest.

Intruder.

I smell you. Against the north wall – the place for the unborn, the suicides, for travellers without names – you, Intruder, have made a den. Your sleeping bag is ugly plastic fibre, cold against my tongue.

The sanctuary was built to be open, always. Holy, holy, holy place: locks unthinkable. Then men came, stripped the roof of its lead, tore down the painted screens, trampled the Dead. I howled and raged, unheeded. When the locks came, I slunk to my den to grieve.

Like you.

Between my teeth, your skull is brittle with loneliness. You sigh, sensing me through the wine that dulls your blood.

My tail droops. I am a poor guardian.

I can't keep you warm, Intruder. But I will keep you company.

|A Little Star|

A lamp with a shade of red paper. No matter what draughty lodge or bawdy house Benjamin laid his head for the night, he saw that Lime Street crimson whenever he closed his eyes, the way another man might see the face of a girl he loved, or a child a ghost in the doorway.

Benjamin followed the Chinese girl up the black lacquered stairs. Xue, her name was. She told him once it meant 'snow'. Or perhaps he dreamt that, floating on the clouds. He could barely see, but he knew the way through each curtained doorway, past sailors and costermongers sprawled on couches thick with cushions. He had read of insects that lived in caves so devoid of light, they were born without eyes. As Xue led him across the landing, Benjamin caught a glimpse of one such creature: Xue's father, clambering like an ancient crab up the stairs to the garret bedroom. When Xue caught him staring, he looked away to the stone Buddha sitting on a side table. The figure was crudely-done, smirking like a Haymarket drunk. Benjamin could have fixed it, once.

His customary couch waited on the third floor where the ceiling billowed with pinned silk. Xue turned her back to hang his coat, and Benjamin's artistic training stirred long enough to sluggishly appraise her beauty. The girl bundled up her black hair with two sharp prongs, like chisels, topped with crescent moons. She could sense him watching her, he knew that, but she didn't fear his kind. He hadn't felt activity in the southern counties for a considerable time.

"Thought you said your farewells," Xue said. "You lose your studio?"

"I decided the rent was an extravagance."

"Clever boy."

Hers was an unbecoming voice for a woman. There was a sphynxy coolness to it that was almost seductive when she gently shook him awake, dry-mouthed and mystified. But now, when he was all anticipation, he wanted to take his shaking hands and strike her.

"Sculpting's no profession," Xue went on. "You make a nice statue, what then? One push, in bits."

She glided away to fetch the pipe, leaving Benjamin alone and miserable. He held out his hands, willing them to be still. Nothing so bitter as a lost gift. Every human figure he created now came out pinched and mean, as if on the seventh day, God rested only because he'd spent the last six drinking. The other Academy students said he was poxy. Little Ben and his Little Problem. Only one thing soothed him, and he could taste it already, wafting in from other rooms where those lucky men lay stupefied.

His longings were interrupted when a broad fellow in a docker's overcoat ducked through the beaded curtain. His cap brushed the billowing ceiling, and before Benjamin could do anything to avoid it, the stranger was upon him with a hearty handshake. "Bit of daylight wouldn't go amiss in here," he said, dumping himself onto the adjacent couch. "Winchester, sir. Of Deptford."

Men did not offer their names in places such as this. In the red glower of the lamps, Benjamin eyed Winchester's hands, smothered in anchors and compasses. Good hands. The sort that did their master's bidding.

When Benjamin failed to respond, the stranger was not offended. "You'll forgive me my enthusiasm, sir, but I have sorely missed the company of Englishmen. Until this morning, I hadn't set foot on these shores for twenty years."

Jesus wept, he was trapped with a talker. Benjamin glanced out into the hall for any sign of Xue and her sharp hairsticks. Perhaps it wasn't too late to take a couch downstairs.

Nevertheless, best to be polite to a man twice one's size. "Twenty years is a long time to be away, Mister Winchester."

"I said as much to the judge, but it was that or the rope, and I've always had a nose for a bargain. Transportation, mate. Life in Australia. Not to be sneered at, a journey like that."

That explained the smell of bilgewater. "And now you want to celebrate, I take it?"

Winchester smiled. "No, sir. What I want is of no importance."

He was here to rob people. Well, Benjamin thought, blow you. He had nothing left to be stolen. Only the money in his pockets, and Xue would take that before giving him the pipe. Where in God's name was she? A cramp in his innards caught Benjamin by surprise, and he brought his knees up in pain. Noisily, he breathed through his nose, trying to suck up some vestige of stale smoke hanging in the air, until the wave passed.

When he opened his eyes, the room was rippling gently. Winchester was gazing at him with odd sympathy.

The shakes weren't the half of it. In nine months, Benjamin's weight had almost halved. Elbows and knees rubbed raw as easily as petals. A student from the medical school adjacent to the Academy once told him gin-fiends' organs were pristine and pickled when you opened them up. Benjamin wondered what an anatomist might make of him when the time came. He would sign himself over today if in return they could promise him the steadiness of his blasted hands and a day alone with a chisel and some stone.

Winchester was fiddling with the paper lampshade, lifting it with his inky fingers. Benjamin watched as the stranger reached inside his coat and took out something to warm in front of the flame.

"Nice bit of glass," Benjamin remarked.

"Oh, she isn't glass," said Winchester. "She is my little star."

The stone cast rainbow constellations around the room.

"My life was a string of curses," Winchester said. "But no longer, thanks to her."

Benjamin knew Australia had much to offer in the way of precious stones. Opal. Bloody garnet. Nephrite Jade, rippled green like rotting mutton. Many were suited to the craft of the sculptor, and many more were valuable, but Benjamin did not recognise Winchester's little star as any of these.

Still, if it *was* valuable, this thug plainly wouldn't know it. Benjamin reached for the stone. "May I?"

Winchester considered him. How pathetic he must have seemed, a young man crumpled up like a used handkerchief, the need for the pipe ground into his face like dirt. *You should have seen me last year*, Benjamin wanted to tell him. *You should have seen my commissions. I was magnificent. I was—*

Winchester solemnly shook his head. "With regret, sir, the lady declines."

He placed the stone before him on the low table, allowing Benjamin to look and nothing more. It wasn't a diamond, he could tell that much through the film of second-hand smoke. But there was something star-like about it. An ancient quality, fathomless and cold, not unlike Xue's voice.

"You mean to sell it?"

"*Her*. And not on your life, sir. My little star brought me home. She knew I longed for it, and she did her work for me." Winchester shrugged off his overcoat, letting it crumple stiffly beside him on the cherry blossom cushions. To Benjamin, it seemed two figures sat before him.

"And now," said Winchester. "I must part with her."

The stone glimmered like fresh February ice. Benjamin saw Winchester in the baking Australian desert, filling the years plotting against the judge who sent him there. The sun could cook a man's brain like an egg. Perhaps those tattooed hands were out of practice. Perhaps Winchester needed a helpless little opium eater's neck to get him in the mood.

But he couldn't stop staring at that stone.

"If you don't intend to sell her, what's stopping you giving her to me?"

"She does not want you, sir. Don't take it to heart. She left her former man for me, and she will leave me for whoever takes her fancy. She's a forthright little star."

"And she told you to come to Lime Street."

"I'm a good husband. I do as the lady tells me."

Here, Winchester looked up and smiled. Xue had entered, with a tray and a pipe.

Benjamin was already on his side, reaching like a baby in a crib. "Were you fetching it from China?"

She set down the tray without looking at him. "The gentleman first. Then you."

For a second, Benjamin forgot to breathe. Winchester pressed his money into Xue's hand. They stayed like that for a moment, eye-to-eye, hand in hand, as if betrothed. But Winchester's lady was leaving him, Benjamin said to himself. The thought echoed around his head. Desert sand, tattooed fingers, and the boundless stretch of the sea.

Once, it was said that Benjamin's hands could make marble sing. If he could only touch the little star, just for a moment… Just to remind himself of his old power…

Man alive, he needed a puff.

Still Xue carried out her duties with infuriating leisure. Benjamin's voice rose unsteadily: "I was here first. Are you listening, you yellow dog? I shan't pay if you—"

"Oh, all your money."

She was laughing at him. Oh, but he was too sick to go upstairs and yell at her crippled father. Benjamin lay there, aching with envy as Xue prepared the pipe and the pillows for Winchester, arranging the red lamp to warm the resin in the bowl. When her work was done, she dipped a small bow. In the girl's cupped hands, the little star winked. Servant, queen, goddess of abundance and mercy. Benjamin tasted sweat. The stone disappeared into Winchester's waistcoat, and Xue slid from the room like a shadow.

Benjamin shuffled towards the edge of his couch. "I say. Winchester. Do a fellow a favour? One little puff to tide me over. You can take one from mine in return, but I simply… would highly appreciate…"

Had he even spoken out loud? Winchester's huge body had already surrendered to the opium's magic. Xue was right. It wasn't simply the loss of the studio. Someone had to pay his Academy fees. Someone had to pay for this. And if Benjamin was honest to himself, he knew which he would crawl for, given the choice. That short deliverance. That dependable peace.

Yes.

He swayed over the sleeping man, poised with his hand over Winchester's heart. Layers of stiff linen and wool, and nestling somewhere inside, a mere Australian rock. But he salivated for it. The odour of Winchester's body tainted the sweetness of the opium, and the need in Benjamin leapt painfully, sending a deep shudder through his useless hands. His fingers glanced against Winchester's waistcoat, and there it was, the little star, like a teardrop in his hand.

So much for the lady not wanting him. Benjamin swept up his coat and hat. Winchester lay still, breathing peacefully in the crimson gloom while his pipe smouldered away, sinfully neglected.

Benjamin was kissing it goodbye before he knew it. The smoke rolled through his body and he grabbed the edge of the table to steady himself. In his moment of pleasure, the proximity of the lamp was irrelevant. It toppled back towards the couch, and Benjamin watched in fuzzy disbelief as the red paper shade was consumed in a languid heartbeat.

There is a foolhardy quantity of fabric in this room, Benjamin said to himself. Sprawled on the floor, he had a capital view as the silks pinned to the ceiling began to undulate under the rising flames. Winchester, the sluggard, slept on, even as the couch went up and the stone in Benjamin's hand quickened with heat like a living thing.

In bushfire season, the snakes leave their sandy burrows, and make for the towns en masse.

One of Xue's brothers was charging up the stairs. Benjamin found himself on his feet, barrelling past, knocking over the side table with the smiling stone Buddha. As Benjamin fled past dark doorways, the most lucid denizens of Lime Street began to stir. As the smoky air thickened, someone cried 'fire', and he heard a shriek that must have been Xue's. He found her trying to fight a path up the stairs as he and half a dozen men came thundering down, shoeless and bewildered. Knots of snakes, twisting their way to safety.

Xue grabbed Benjamin's wrist. "Help me up."

'Up' was nothing but death. Unlike Winchester, he would keep his little star safe.

Out on the cobbles, Benjamin fell on his knees, coughing and rubbing at his smarting eyes. He caught a handful of water from the Lime Street pump, and with the stone in his mouth, swallowed hard. Knowing his opium-eater's guts, he wouldn't be seeing her again for two weeks.

He lurched away towards the nearest alley, but as he dodged a carriage he could not resist one last look at his old hideout. The top half of the house was engulfed. All that opium. The hideous waste. He felt he should salute, or say a short prayer, but when he shielded his eyes to look at the attic bedroom, he saw a spindly something flailing in the blaze.

He had quite forgotten Xue's antique father. And so, it appeared, had everyone else. As the old man clawed at the window, Benjamin's whole sorry body begged him to run. He didn't want such an image in his dreams.

Down the alley, he collapsed beside a child's hopscotch grid. A piece of chalk lay abandoned, and out of habit he began to draw. Aimless swirls to calm himself, a crude flower, his own name. At first, he didn't understand how he was holding the chalk steady. It usually took a whole bowl and a four hour sleep to reliably grip a teaspoon. Hardly daring to breathe, he sketched a smiling face, a skyline, a woman's profile. He was laughing like a drunk, but for the first time in memory, he was wide awake and fully seated in his body. It was all his again: hands and feet to enjoy and put to work. It was the little star. She hadn't wanted Winchester, the filthy rogue. She hadn't *wanted* whichever man had come before. All this time, while Benjamin suffered, she was making her way across deserts and oceans, passing hand to hand… to him.

Benjamin wasn't alone.

Xue's face shone. One of her hairsticks had given way, leaving a coil of black to sway in the smoky wind. Her dress was a ruin of ash and splinters.

Benjamin rushed to her. "Xue! My hands, look at them. It's a miracle. I'll draw your portrait. Look."

Xue stepped towards him, dreamy-eyed, and for one gleaming moment Benjamin thought to ask her to marry him. He could take her away from the city, build them a home somewhere green and bright with a studio for him and a nursery for her and their dark-haired children. He put his steady hands on her shoulders. He had the little star. There was nothing that couldn't be fixed now.

With a hard tug against the suction, Xue slid the long shaft of her hairstick free from the soft place below Benjamin's ribs.

Benjamin looked down. Xue was serenely scissoring two fingers inside him, opening up the layers of clothing and muscle to delve into the cavity within. A soft pop and a glassy glitter. His precious trinket in her slippery hands.

Xue wiped the Lime Street crimson down her dress. "She doesn't want you," she said.

|Veterans|

~

Rookie

Because Dad was a veteran, my name was picked at random to attend the Aristotle Prep School in the Philharmonic Quarter. I was six, excited to take the tram to the pretty end of town where they ate real bread and real chicken, not the spongey imitation stuff our ration coupons guaranteed. The school was a picture book château to me, a confection of arches and spires untouched by the bombing. I'd learn Latin there, and the Classics, and a lot of other dusty old things Mum said people would want now the war was over. People could only watch so many drone strikes before deciding things were nicer in the Middle Ages, she told me. And then she apologised.

Even at six years old I was built like a stork, but you couldn't tell what was going on underneath, not unless you were a highly specialised geneticist. To the selection board, I was just another buck-toothed kid, but it took about two hours on my first day for the pecking order to be established. *Generously funded by The Clarion Foundation: proud to give back.* The rich mosaic tapered around the reception hall, and as I craned my neck to admire the trumpets of mirrored glass, a passing boy called me a useless mouth. At break, an older girl took my colouring book and dropped it in the toilet. She'd heard the teachers talking about my funny hands. I needed a special pen, she said, laughing high and sharp.

"It's special because they heard you love to draw," Mum said when I told her. It sounded like another apology.

Charlotte came to Aristotle through the Clarion Foundation's Volunteer Division. Mister Depaul, our hollow-cheeked headmaster, had her read from a storybook that took up her whole lap.

"Warms the heart," he said, patting Charlotte's shoulder where her long hair curled softly. "Children in our enemies' countries have no

"

storybooks at all, isn't that right, Miss Charlotte? Only the texts of their primitive religions."

I watched Charlotte's sweet, round face; the gratitude on her pursed lips. I thought of Dad, flying jets across the sea, and I was proud.

"Miss Charlotte was injured during the war," Mister Depaul told us, his gaunt face the picture of solemnity. "Thanks to the generous intervention of the Clarion Foundation, she is here to read to us today. She's a hard worker. What do we say, girls and boys?"

We knew all the words: *our enemies*, *useless mouths*, and of course the Clarion motto. We sang out in shrill unison: "Proud to give back."

One of Charlotte's legs was synthetic. She always wore wide gingham skirts, and we were forever trying to peep under the cotton and guess which one. She read us pre-war fairy tales after our breakfast of Granny Gertie's Fortified Flakes and authentic boiled eggs from chickens, not a lab. "Once upon a time," she would begin, and someone always giggled. Once upon a time, went the schoolyard joke, Charlotte could wiggle her toes.

My teachers didn't like Charlotte, something I found puzzling. Mister Depaul had explicitly said she wasn't a useless mouth. I saw useless mouths every day in my quarter: bearded men cowering from the rain in shop doorways, calling out for spare change. Dad said they weren't proper veterans, because a true soldier would have some pride. "I'm all banged up too, but you don't hear me complaining," he said, and often. Every Veterans' Day, the government sent him a bunch of red plastic flowers in the mail. His prize, I guessed, for not complaining.

Charlotte never got flowers on Veterans' Day. One of the older kids used a throwaway email to tell everyone there was a tracker under her skin so she couldn't sneak off and join our enemies. Clarion would know if she crossed the school perimeter, and then a bomb inside her would detonate and she'd leave a smoking crater at the gates where our mums picked us up at 3:30. The leg was a distraction, I overheard a girl whisper to a grinning audience. Charlotte was already dead. She'd stepped on a landmine, but Clarion men in rubber suits bolted her back together and added a CPU and a synthetic face. That's why she never reacted when you called her Stumpy.

I was primed to smell the implication, even at that age: Charlotte had been, if not an outright traitor, a kind of quisling. Her loose lips sank ships, as Dad would say. Still, I found it hard to believe. She was pleasantly boring, like a pretty talking doll with a handful of gentle phrases. The three little pigs built three little houses. The dwarves wept for Snow White. But there was, nonetheless, something disjointed about our storyteller. The bullies were right; Charlotte did live at the school. She had a room of her own, with a toilet and a kettle and a window overlooking the car park, and I always assumed she liked it in there. My own bedroom looked out onto a burnt-out parachute factory. That summer, Clarion had covered the ruins in a frame of scaffolding and an enormous canvas sign. *Proud to give back*, it declared, alongside a picture of a girl a little older than me handing a red flower to a smiling man in uniform. When I lay in bed, I could see the girl's clenched fist, each slender digit in perfect proportion, pale and clean. When I grew up, I told myself, I'd have hands like that.

Once, left unsupervised, a group of us ventured down the cold corridor to Charlotte's quarters to listen breathlessly at the door for signs of life, reanimated or otherwise.

I wasn't any better than the others. They were older kids, jumpy and giggling, and if they were laughing at Charlotte, they weren't laughing at me and my funny hands. And yes, I wanted to know what horrors lay behind that door.

"Don't make a noise," one boy whispered, hot against my cheek. "The bomb, remember?"

I was mutely helpless when he gripped me by the shoulders, swung open Charlotte's door and thrust me through it. I flung myself at the door just as it closed in my face, and as I heard the others laughing on the other side there was a very real threat of wetting myself.

"You're not supposed to come in here."

The children went squealing away the moment they heard Charlotte's voice. As my panic peaked, I wondered if the Clarion Foundation men in their rubber suits would bolt the scattered bits of me back together. Would they stretch a blandly smiling latex face over the wreck of my own? How would Mum and Dad recognise me? Perhaps, came an appalling thought, they would prefer me that way. As I squeezed my eyes shut against the unbearable possibilities, hot tears rolled down my chin.

"I'm sorry— I didn't— Please don't—"

"Katy."

Charlotte was sitting in a chair with a cup of tea and a magazine. My heart thumped: *bomb bomb bomb.*

She put down her mug. "Come and get a tissue."

I glanced at her legs, pale under the canopy of her skirt.

"There's no bomb. And I'm not a robot. Look. I eat chocolate digestives like everyone else. You can have one, if you like."

She could see I didn't believe her, so she smoothed her wide gingham skirt until the expanse of it resembled a picnic blanket. It worked maternal magic on me, and I crawled to her, sniffling, and laid my head in her warm lap.

"You should wear rings on those long fingers," she said. She took my hand and examined it. There was so much adult talk of special pens and uncomfortable plastic splints, but no one ever talked about decorating my hands. Some of the older girls wore nail polish to school, and I tried to imagine myself choosing a bottle at the shops with Mum. Lilac, or sparkly silver. No, I couldn't see it.

With great care, Charlotte pushed on my fingertips, bending them up and back to the broken doll angle I did on purpose to make my dad wince. "Does this hurt?" she asked.

"No."

"And when you draw?"

It made me sad to think of it. I already knew I'd never be any good, special pen or otherwise. Daffodils, puppydogs, the mangled steel beams of the parachute factory: everything I tried to draw came out warped and hopeless where my thumb wobbled in its socket.

My head lolled against Charlotte's knee where flesh met thermoplastic, and I felt her flinch. Obtuse child that I was, I only then noticed she was in pain. It wasn't pain like falling off your bike or banging your toe. This looked more like being dragged.

Hadn't Mister Depaul said she was injured in the fighting? The scornful glances of the teachers hinted at something worse. In history class, Mister Watson told us stories. He'd seen a man walk into a supermarket and light it up in blinding flame in an instant. They were jealous of us, our enemies, of our freedom and our comforts. They wanted us to feel terror. Listening to Mister Watson, I did. With my fingers bunched in the cotton of Charlotte's skirt I went to speak, but fear filled my mouth, white hot, and the question remained inside.

Around Charlotte's wrist, her Sensus glowed. I'd taken it to be an ordinary tattoo at story time, but up close I watched the pulsing linework getting to work under her skin, the veins of stickleback blue. Dad said his squadron Sensus released something to keep him awake on night exercises, but the Air Force deactivated it when the war ended, which was why he snored in his chair after dinner. The only others I'd seen were on the people queuing outside our neighbourhood Clarion Clinic; poorly people, people who needed medicine for a long time, maybe even forever. Dad didn't like people looking at his Sensus. They might get the wrong impression, he said. He wasn't a useless mouth.

I should have left – I wasn't supposed to be there, after all – but the tattoo held my attention, pulsing slower now, cruising to a halt. I watched the little wrinkles around Charlotte's mouth slacken as the chemicals flowed over her like a soothing breeze in the stuffy little room.

I touched her, silently asking if she was okay. When Charlotte's gaze eventually found me, her smile was big and gauzy, like when Mum had a second glass of wine with our Sunday roast.

"They top it up with morphine once a month, if I'm good," she sighed.

"Will it make you better?"

"No, Katy. No, I'm as well as I'll ever be." Charlotte's smile wavered. She blinked and blinked again as if abruptly remembering where she was. Her voice, so musical and sweet at story time, sounded strange to me, frayed at the edges. "When they patched me up, they... They measured my body and took scans of my face and they said... They said I had the perfect attributes – that's how they put it, *perfect* – for working with the nation's most valuable assets. That's you. So here I am, reading fables to children. All my accomplishments, all my misdemeanours, swept aside. A good little Clarion volunteer."

I didn't know that word: *misdemeanour*. I knew *air raid*, *attack*, *dogfight*. I knew Saturday morning cartoons where our brave heroes in uniform vanquished the invading masses again and again. I knew *sanction* and *blockade*, the reasons Mum's Sunday roasts never quite filled me up. I knew my place at Aristotle Prep was a special privilege, something that could never take place in an enemy country. The Clarion Foundation made sure I was educated, despite my scuffed shoes and my special pen. I didn't like the way Charlotte said 'Clarion', like the name of a bully you hated but were too weak to fight. I knew that feeling, but the strange association set a gnawing in my stomach.

"Miss Charlotte…?"

Her soft hand on the back of my neck. "No, sweetheart," she said, and reached for her storybook. "How about I tell you a nicer story?"

Dispatches

I got my Sensus on my eighteenth birthday. It could easily be mistaken for an ankle chain, but in my office trousers it's completely covered and that's how I prefer it. It releases a beta blocker for my heart at breakfast and dinner, and an SSRI for pain about half an hour before I go to bed. I queue at the clinic once a month to have the ink replenished with my prescriptions. My Sensus doesn't light up. Dad sacrificed our savings to make sure I had the discreet kind, the kind that tingles warmly when they're booting up.

Mine looks like the perforated film seals you get around the tops of jars. I wish I could have designed my own, but even if I was any good as an artist, it's not an option. The patterns are randomised to prevent duplication. Clarion cracks down hard on piracy.

I would love to say I spent the years after Aristotle Prep using art to see my body in a kindly light, but when I slip on my finger splints and attempt to sketch my bust, my eyes follow the faultlines, the fractures that threaten to bring the whole structure down. I could spend hours rendering my collarbones delicate as feathers, or turning my freckled skin into a pixie canvas of constellations, but all the while I'd be thinking of the time an old boyfriend told me he could pour a shot of vodka into the deep hollow of my sternum and call it a Katy Cocktail.

I'd have a new scar, soon enough. My annual check-up showed developments in my heart. I told Dad not to worry. We knew this was coming, the natural progression of things. The cardiologist had given me a couple of weeks to think about my options, which realistically boiled down to a public clinic with worn linoleum and a grinding waiting list. The big city private hospitals weren't for the likes of me. I intended to spend the wait silent and stoic, no trouble to anyone. Still, I couldn't help but feel I'd let Dad down.

Then the letter arrived.

I stood in the hallway of my shared flat, staring at the stiff cream envelope under the stuttering fluorescent light the landlord kept promising to replace. A paper letter, with a stamp. How quaintly archaic. Why not go the whole hog and send a carrier pigeon?

"It has come to the attention of The Clarion Foundation's Volunteer Division…"

How had it come to their attention? I hadn't taken a day off for the appointment, just moved my shifts around. Someone must have seen me take the hospital shuttle and fancied claiming a tasty Clarion finder's fee. I thought about Margaret who does the admin. A gossip, always telling me to try yoga or cider vinegar. Then there was Ellen in Accounts. Ellen's epileptic stepsister was with the Volunteer Division, and Ellen was forever going on about how good it was for her to be giving back after getting her brain implant. She was sent to help in a Veteran's Club somewhere up north, if I remember rightly. Ellen called it hostess work, but I wasn't sure what that meant and didn't want to make a spectacle of myself by asking.

Volunteers. They faded into the scenery, they were so ubiquitous: girls in powerchairs greeting shoppers at supermarket entrances; old women with titanium knees pouring coffee at motorway service stations; the white-haired young guy outside my local tram depot handing out Clarion leaflets promising a new age of civic pride. I don't know his story – we've never talked – but presumably he enjoys himself out there.

Too much standing made my head spin, so whatever I volunteered for, it would have to be sedentary. Reading stories to horrible children, like Charlotte. I hadn't given Charlotte a thought for years. I remembered the Foundation's saccharine infomercials: smiling young women pushing prams while men held doors and doffed their caps. "People were friendlier before the war," Dad would admonish me when I rolled my eyes. "You knew your neighbours in those days. Kids minded their Ps and Qs. This lot are bringing all that back."

Wholesome scenery, benign as cardboard.

I told the kettle to make me a cup of tea and returned to the letter. The Clarion trumpet sigil was watermarked into the paper, and I worried at it with my thumbnail. Oh Jesus, motivational appearances. They'd have me smiling on civic stages while an official in a twinset exhibited me to young graduates. *The only disability is a bad attitude.* These days, all the glossy magazines were touting that wartime bootstraps-and-stiff-upper-lip dogma, tarted up until it resembled a lifestyle. I'd used a stack of them to paper over Dad's windows last winter when he thought enemy satellites were watching his front room again.

I needed heart surgery; I didn't have time for this twee shit. I was yet to see the small print, but it was like Mum always said: with my bendy joints, I could wriggle out of anything. If Clarion wanted a fresh volunteer, they were out of luck.

I took the train to the government's Bureau of Help in the neighbouring quarter. Probably paranoid to travel so far, but I didn't want Margaret or Ellen spotting me and making a soap opera out of it. The damp autumn was draining into winter, and my ankles were upset about it, but when I got to the tram link there was a chain across the gate and a swinging sign already festooned in graffiti: CLOSED. For months, by the looks of it. I swore under my pluming breath. There was no room for my braces inside my smart shoes, so it took a long, sore hour to trudge to the Bureau, wedged behind one of those multi-storey family restaurants offering the genuine farmhouse pub experience. Clarion-owned, I realised, judging by the trumpets etched into the front door. I'd never stopped to wonder how far the Foundation's tendrils stretched.

"So, it's elective surgery?"

The Bureau girl worked her painted lips around each ambiguous syllable. *El-ec-tive.*

"My mum died on the waiting list." It was just words at this point. I couldn't allow it to be anything more.

The Bureau girl took her stylus and stabbed at her screen, angled just out of sight. I imagined my life condensed to a series of check marks on a government database, to a circled score between one and ten. I found I couldn't meet the Bureau girl's eyes.

"And you walked here?" she asked.

"Yes, from the station. It's—"

Her eyes darted to her screen. "You mentioned pain when walking."

"It varies. I can only do so much before—"

A burst of typing shut me up.

"There's a Bureau in your own quarter," she said. "More convenient, surely?"

I felt a flush creep over my cheeks. She wasn't accusing me of fakery, I realised. She only thought I was stupid.

"And have your doctors indicated a time period for this surgery?"

"It can't wait. Early next year."

The daffodils would be coming up. I'd miss all that, being shut inside. My flatmates would have to bring the bed downstairs for me so I could shuffle to the toilet. I could make a huge batch of Bolognese and freeze it in little bags. I could still be self-sufficient. I could, as far as possible, avoid being a burden.

The Bureau girl had pretty nails, and they sped over her keyboard as she recorded my response. "With your patchy employment history, your procedure will need to take place at a taxpayer-funded facility. And then there's the matter of rehab, follow-ups, maybe even further surgical intervention – chronic conditions like yours take a toll on the public purse. The Clarion Foundation has always been a tremendous help in bolstering the government's endeavours with their secondary labour market programmes, and all they ask in return is that people who will continue to put strain on the taxpayer—"

I felt my lips give an involuntary twitch. *Useless mouths.*

"—contribute to society elsewhere. You're not the only one. And Clarion never makes you do anything you're uncomfortable with."

I was uncomfortable. I was distinctly fucking uncomfortable.

"But it's voluntary, right? It's in the name," I pressed her. "I have to agree."

Her long fingernails struck the desk. "Really, the Foundation asks for so little. Don't forget: our parents' generation had the draft."

She slid a tablet towards me. On the screen was the unflattering photograph from my office security pass, plus boxes to tick: a list of skills and interests. The options were a joke – typical HR drivel – as if data entry and waitressing were anyone's passions. Feeling my temper fraying, I smudged a thumbprint next to half a dozen at random and pushed the tablet away.

"Do you play any instruments?" As she filed away the tablet in the desk drawer, the girl appeared pacified, but still her eyes flicked dubiously over the splints on my fingers. "There's a Clarion lady who plays piano at the Signet Memorial Plaza, Monday to Thursdays. It's great for the veterans. Perhaps you could have a chat, let her put you into a more positive frame of mind."

"How long has she been there?"

The girl shrugged. Years, then. I tried not to envision years. I had to hold it together.

"I like the job I have." It wasn't true, but the statement came out with a crack in the middle.

"And you can have it back. Once you've paid your debts."

In the walkway between ShoeZone and the Vitashake stand, a bronze likeness of General Signet glared at the ceiling lights with heroic determination. Someone had laid a bundle of plastic poppies at his feet, almost covering the pale square where the Veteran's Aid donation box had been ripped away.

I followed the trill of a piano to the food court where a woman in a hoochy approximation of an army uniform held sway.

"Now then, who knows this one? All together now... *There'll be bluebirds over...*"

Half the sparse audience were too young to remember the war. There was a cleaner taking a break, three nannies with a brace of toddlers each, and a pack of sniggering teenagers sat at the back, scoffing chips. I took a seat at the edge, feeling my ankles sigh in relief.

The singer had a record out. She couldn't be with Clarion: strictly non-profit for volunteers. I looked over her shoulder at the pianist, an older woman crammed into a nightmare of khaki wool and brass buttons teamed with a low-cut satin blouse. She played well, but her smile was all lip gloss, red as a plastic poppy. The longer I sat listening to ditties about sweethearts and submarines, the more I found myself staring at the pianist's all-too-perfect right leg and remembering a school day, long ago, when I crept down a corridor where I didn't belong.

I waited for the set to end before making my approach.

"So, should I salute, or...?"

The pianist looked up through false eyelashes. I tried to see her as she was at school, all crisp and minty like Julie Andrews. Seeing her older and heavier in a push-up bra made me want to avert my eyes. She didn't remember me.

"Hey there, doll," Charlotte said brightly. "Veronica will be back in a jiffy with more tunes from the golden age of—"

I held out my hand. I pushed on my fingertips, bent my wrist into the broken doll angle Dad hated so much. "Turns out this *is* meant to hurt."

Charlotte's face remained friendly, but her voice dropped.

"I have another hour here, then I'm answering phones at the exchange until nine." She stole a glance at the singer, obliviously signing CDs for some pensioners with shopping bags swinging on their arms. "Can you make it up to the flats by the old aircraft hangers?"

"Those are flats?" I'd taken them for derelict, looking out from the train.

The pensioners were taking seats. Charlotte inflicted a tremendous, vacant smile at me and pumped my hand. "Thanks, doll. CDs are waiting for you by the table, and even some download codes for the grandkids, too. V for victory!"

I took the cue. I had enough coupons in my purse for some of those chips the teenagers were enjoying. As I settled in the food court with my greasy supper, my Sensus warmed up to release my early evening medication. It'll all be alright, I told myself. But when I thought of Charlotte's costume, I screwed up my chip papers and threw them in the bin. They weren't even real potato.

The path to the flats was lit by a series of mildewy globes set so far apart, I nearly strayed into the dark bushes twice. It was an ideal place for a maniac to lurk, I thought, fighting nervousness. Still, being murdered would undeniably get me out of volunteering.

She was waiting for me at the door, finishing a cigarette. I was relieved to see she'd ditched the costume, though this wasn't any

Charlotte I'd seen before. If anything, these were a man's clothes adding defensive inches to her frame. Her Sensus was lit up around her wrist, brighter than any street light.

"I still have chocolate digestives," she said.

Her flat was lit in an eerie blue light from a source I couldn't pinpoint. I think it was a security thing, to make it look like she was in when she wasn't. A muffled dispute was underway next door, but Charlotte had made the little place comfortable: she had a fish tank with a few solar-powered guppies, a bookshelf crammed with paperbacks, and a kitchenette well-stocked with ersatz teas and novelty mugs. *Coffee, chocolate, men… some things are better rich!*

The six-year-old in me was amazed when my old storyteller offered me a beer. When Charlotte took a sip, the Sensus around her wrist gave a hectoring throb. She saw me looking and shrugged.

"Clarion. They know where I am, if I'm awake or asleep. I don't work with children anymore, so I can have a drink once in a while without getting a visit from Mother Superior. Watch this."

On the bookshelf was an infra-red flashlight, the kind used by rat catchers to illuminate their quarry's tracks. Charlotte turned the red beam on her arm. There, glowing over fibrous arrangements of muscle and blood vessels, was a flickering string of digits. Her balance, I realised with a jolt of nausea. As the Bureau of Help girl put it, her *debt*.

"Bloody hell. I didn't know they did that."

"They don't put it in the brochure, no." Charlotte sloshed her beer around her teeth. "Interest, all of it. I can't leave the country, I can't take out a mortgage, I can't so much as auction an old couch without informing them of my earnings and giving them a cut. Same goes for inheritance, if I had anyone left to bequeath me anything. Love life? Forget it. If anyone were reckless enough to marry me, they'd automatically be co-responsible for my debt. And by telling you this, I've violated my NDA, so I'll thank you to keep that to yourself."

I sat down on her deflated couch. When my jeans rode up, my own Sensus peeked out, and she clocked it instantly.

"That's a nice one. Paid for?"

"My mum left me and my dad some money. Better than having to remember to carry a bag of pills everywhere, you know?"

"But now you're here with me, making that face."

"Wet tissue paper." I took a long swig. "That's what the doctor said. All my insides. I need a Microscaf procedure on my aorta, or I'm going to—" I licked my lips where the foam was bitterest. "I have a minimum wage job, no insurance, no house to re-mortgage…"

"And you don't want to end up in a shopping centre, wearing a costume and calling people 'doll'."

She wasn't sneering. She could see all I wanted was to lay my head in her lap and whine. Unlike me, Charlotte had a life before Clarion. I had caught a glimpse of it, long ago. I felt a flicker of that childhood fear now, like nudging open a door you knew you should leave closed.

"Charlotte, how were you injured?"

I watched as she used her sleeve to wipe away the vestiges of lipstick cracked in the corner of her mouth. I realised I'd rarely seen Charlotte without a painted smile.

"Before war was declared, before you were born, we had a laboratory," she said quietly. "Just me, a couple of Swedes, three Nigerians, and a gorgeous Frenchmen – André, my boyfriend. I was making a cup of coffee, I remember, in our little kitchenette. I was spooning in the sugar when they walked in – three of them, in balaclavas. The coffee saved me, I think. They took me for someone unimportant, just a tea lady. But then André in his lab coat asked them what they wanted, always direct to a fault. He died first. I never heard from the other survivors again. The doctors told me they'd gone home to their respective countries. War was inevitable, the news kept telling us, and foreigners were getting out while they could. But I just knew…" Blinking, she watched the plastic fish bumping around in their tank. "I lost a leg, and the other hasn't been right since."

Whatever I'd been expecting, it wasn't this. Even now, I'd undervalued Charlotte, and she met my chastened look with a shrug.

"Terrorists," I said in quiet awe. "At Aristotle, Mister Watson, he told us—"

Charlotte huffed into her bottle. "Fables. There were attacks, but as for our jealous enemies sneaking into banks and universities every weekend and shooting them up for sport?" She paused, running her piano-playing fingers through the condensation beading on the glass. "You were little, Katy. You only have what they told you."

I felt small again, always left out of the joke. "But why would someone attack scientists if they weren't… what? Foreign agents? Terrorists? What did they want?"

"We were working on subdermal pharmaceutical delivery. Intelligent ink."

The floor tilted. I was drunker than I thought. "You mean Sensus ink?"

She made a face like I'd just compared her baby to my Chihuahua. "Your Sensus was put there by a Clarion employee with a tattoo gun and Pound signs in his eyes. Our plan was to give that tool to you. Say you're a mother in Siberia. Your baby needs her first vaccinations. Your older child is insulin-dependent, your back is playing up, and the doctor is miles away through deep snow. What if one pen could do it all? The ink knows, it thinks, it adapts. It seeks out the source of pain. A Sensus does only as much as it's told; it requires constant replenishment. Our pen could brew up medications from the body's own waste products, or download a recipe from the cloud, no different from growing synthetic eggs in a lab and frying them for breakfast. It could buy you time after a car accident, or if a drone's taken out the local hospital. Release trapped fluid, hold together torn flesh…"

She paused, lips working silently as she pushed a memory aside.

"The plan was to go open source – free, fair, worldwide. We were so close." Charlotte sat with me on the sagging sofa, and with my permission she took my hand in hers. "You have a connective tissue disorder. What if you could make your own orthotics out of synthetic collagen? Just take the pen and draw your own wrist brace, tracing the pattern the pain has lit up for you. The ink swims down through your skin and holds you, gently, on a cellular level. No dislocations, no conspicuous neoprene. No one would give you looks at the bus stop and offer advice."

I gave an involuntary snort. "Fucking yoga."

Charlotte smiled tightly. "They took everything. All our research, all our prototypes. The University withdrew our funding, closed the lab. No one would tell me why. It took months for me to recover, to walk again, to sleep, but thanks to the Clarion Foundation, my doctors could offer me the very latest in subdermal pharmaceutical technology to treat the pain: the Sensus. A shoddy imitation of the work my friends died for. I spent the war alone, sewing uniforms, packing rations – a little volunteer work to pay for my treatment. I wasn't a traitor, but what I'd done at the lab, some might say… not sufficiently patriotic." In the weak light, her eyes shone. "Clarion sent the gunmen. They couldn't have us distributing for free what they could withhold for a profit."

We sat in silence. There were no family photos in Charlotte's flat. No postcards from friends on the fridge. In another Universe, Charlotte would have a sleek laboratory in the city, and I wouldn't even know her. I could be using her pen on myself in the bathroom mirror. Wonky geometry was all I could manage, but it would be enough, tracing my aorta down through its warped enclosure, willing it to be strong. And after that – living. Authentic tedious pre-war living, just like everyone else.

My Sensus tingled. It was warming up, ready to release the evening's medication. That prickling sensation, once so benign, now signalled Clarion's presence under my skin, the hold they already had on me. In my tipsy distress I reached for the infra-red flashlight on the coffee table.

Charlotte tried to stop me, but she was as clumsy as I was, slopping her beer, as I rolled down my sock and turned the beam on my ankle.

There it was, swimming inside me.

Something clogged my throat.

A number. A long one. My debt.

Charlotte was still. "Are you quite sure you didn't agree to anything?"

Panic sent an opioid tremor through my brain. I retraced that morning at the Bureau of Help. The girl's cool insistence. Her pretty, painted fingers pushing a tablet across the table, wordlessly asking for the thumbprint I freely gave.

I grabbed at Charlotte's bulky sweater. "How do I make it go away?"

"You can't."

I jumped to my feet. Pain, stupid predictable pain. "A knife. We can cut it out."

"I'm sorry."

"I only went to the Bureau of Help."

"They're not there to help *us*, Katy. We're a labour source. Another army."

I fell back down beside her. There was nowhere to put the rage. A burning pressure mounted in my ribcage, a bomb I could no longer contain. All that stopped me from sounding the siren and wailing out loud was Charlotte beside me, smelling of synthetic hops and makeup remover, radiating wordless sympathy.

"I don't know what I— what I came here for, I—" I felt a sob raising its hackles inside my chest and swallowed it down with everything I had. "I'm sorry. I'm being a nuisance. I don't know what I was thinking—"

I was struggling to my feet again when Charlotte's warm hand pressed me gently back down.

There was no gingham skirt to smooth over her thighs, no oversized storybook. I lay my head on her hard thermoplastic knee.

"I think," she ventured, "you were hoping to find a comrade."

|Kindness at the Four Boars Inn|

With thanks to David Southwell.

It took the pot boy three days to die, once the gentlemen departed the Four Boars Inn.

Anna was not a girl given to tears. Tears cost strength, and that commodity was firmly the property of Mister Beale and his inn; for the lighting of the bedroom fires, for the emptying of the chamber pots and the scrubbing of the grout between the tap room tiles. But as she stood amongst the ash trees on the wrong side of the churchyard wall, the maid-of-all-work permitted herself a moment of stillness.

Ted, sixteen, was the smallest cog in the Four Boars Coaching Inn. Ted's was the only position at the inn Anna didn't envy. The ostlers worked in the open air, Missus Swinney could feast on scraps, but Ted? His life was a scurry of fetching, fixing, and 'Coming, sir!' He was always 'coming, sir'. At that quiet moment, it seemed to Anna that Ted had been called to his grave.

The gentlemen came in the night. It was as if they waited for Anna to settle on her hard wooden bed and slide into a stupor before galloping in with all hell in tow, demanding sherry and supper, bootblack and laundry. The July night was too fierce for anything but fitful dozing. All along the barren highway, the slow worms and the nightjars kept their silent counsel amongst the tinder-dry gorse. The ostlers swept over the horses while Anna presented herself with a sloppy curtsey. The gentlemen ignored her. Three were rickety old fellows, stepping down from the carriage with stately care. The fourth skipped down like a fox leaving a henhouse. As Ted unloaded the luggage, he pressed a coin into the boy's palm, winning one of Ted's smiles, wide and true.

"Four beds," the gentleman said. "If you'll be so kind."

As Anna went down to the kitchen for the second-best glasses, Missus Swinney was lighting the lamps.

"Bit early for the Puck Fair, this lot," she remarked. "But did you see the fat one's watch? That's quality."

"Quality," Anna muttered through a yawn.

The gentlemen booked in for several nights. Mister Hawley the ostler said the leader went by the name of Dabster.

"From up country, if you ask me," Ted said, hauling firewood for the stove. "The *Right Honourable* Misters This, That, and The Other."

Rose sneered. "Father, Son, and the Holy bleedin' Ghost for all I care." How could he be so chirpy at this ungodly hour? Mister Beale, Anna noted sourly, remained in bed. Landlord's privilege, but he was a monster on anything less than eight hours a night. On a good day, he'd rise at seven and stalk into the fields with his rifle to reconcile every living creature he met with their Maker. A bad morning was largely the same, though he carried out his daily slaughter screaming about the French and how they did for his brother at Talavera. Why pile aboard a ship and sail away to war, Anna wondered, when there was so much sweat and blood to be shed at home?

"Dabster tipped me," Ted said, showing off a coin. "Be sweet. You could do with a new bonnet. For the fair."

"What's wrong with my old bonnet, you little shitlark?"

Missus Swinney shut Anna up with a clip round the ear. "Get a move on. Open the bedrooms. Ted! Service."

Take the money, take the food orders, clean the carriage. Anna found the four gentlemen settled in the tap room. One thin, one fat, one short, one tall, like something from a nursery rhyme. The elderly trio were a fright. The highway robbers must have let them go unmolested out of pity.

Dabster, by comparison, was a rogue if ever Anna saw one. She'd never liked a man with a good suit and dirty fingernails.

"Here she is, a true rose of the heathland!" Dabster cried, his jowls jiggling. "What are these rumours I hear of a freshly slaughtered pig?"

"Plenty of gravy," said the frailest man, who looked as if his last meal was some time before the Civil War. "And a second sherry wouldn't go amiss."

Ted cut the carcass, his hair stuck to his shining brow and his knuckles lined in blood. Missus Swinney dropped a dish of gravy, and everyone swore.

"Don't forget the carriage," Anna said, wiping gravy from her shoes. "Dabster said something about a heavy package."

"It could wait," said Missus Swinney. "They'll be going to bed soon, I 'spect."

"Nothing waits," Ted said, and brought the cleaver down with a dull thump. He smiled through a yawn.

You're a pigeon, Anna thought. *Three in the morning, up again in two hours, and you grin?*

When Anna took them their chops and mash, the four gentlemen were filling their pipes. A dwindling supply of tobacco was spread out on the table, flakes of black, and they were picking at it as Anna put their plates down.

"Have a care!" cried Dabster, though he wasn't half so horrified as his aged companions. A flurry of flakes had fallen to the floor, and they all bent to gather them, every black scrap. "That is a valuable commodity."

Anna gave her best impression of giving a tuppenny damn, but before she could extract herself, the tallest gentleman caught her apron. "A fever gripped this area this past winter, is that correct?"

Anna thought back to Christmas. Yes, more funerals than usual. But the inn was far enough from the walls of Coreham for it not to worry her. At least in death you could have a lie down.

"You were untouched?" the short one asked. He had a pocket book and pencil, and a pair of spectacles with glass as thick as Anna's thumb.

"I am well, sir."

"Not you," snapped Mister Tall. "The inn. The staff."

"The pot boy," added his emaciated companion, shoveling potato through his parched lips. He grimaced. "This gravy has lumps in it."

"My venerable colleagues command a certain renown in the world of science," Dabster explained. "The county is a tricksy place for contagions, I have explained to them. Insects, marshland fogs, and whatnot. My companions hypothesise that country folk are hardier than their city cousins."

Sweating and gritty-eyed, Anna bit the inside of her cheek. The hard clarity of winter seemed a hundred years ago.

"You'll find the same with draft horses," said Mister Short. "And certain species of bird. Only last year, I read a wonderfully engaging pamphlet on the effects of ingesting the bone marrow of a Hookland wildcat versus your common London tabby. As a tonic. A pick-me-up."

Was he teasing her? Anna kept her eyes on the flagstones, her face neutral.

"Will that be all, sirs?"

When was the answer ever 'yes'?

~

"Ted! They want you."

Out in the relative cool of the coach house, Anna wiped her brow with her pinny. The pot boy knelt on the carriage steps, looking in.

"Sooner they talk to you, sooner they go to bed," Anna added.

Ted said nothing.

"For pity's sakes, Ted, I haven't the patience."

He turned. In his hands was a great black helmet with a visor and a beaky nose.

"What's it for?" he said.

"How should I bloody know? I have to ready the bedrooms."

Ted stared at the helmet, like a cannonball in his hands. "Anna?"

"What?"

"It smells like…"

A drop of sweat seeped through her eyelashes, stinging salt. "Like nasty old men?"

"No." He ran his finger around the inner rim, picking up a sooty residue. He raised it to his nose, and for a second Anna thought he intended to lick it. "It smells… good?"

Anna walked away without another word. When she looked back, Ted was still kneeling there with the helmet, swaying slightly, as if he could feel a cool breeze blowing only for him.

~

There was no point returning to bed. Through the muggy dawn, Anna scrubbed the kitchen floor of pig's blood. Her head pulsed with giddy exhaustion. Even the hens were abed, giving barely a chuckle as she pilfered their warm eggs.

"Chin up, our Annie."

Ted was bringing up water from the well. That queer, dreamy look had gone, replaced by his customary good cheer.

"I'll push you in," she said.

"I could grow weary of your unrelenting jollity, miss." Ted took a drink and bid her do the same. She let it roll coolly over her tongue, tasting faintly of heather. At last years' Puck Fair, Ted had bobbed for apples in a barrel, dunking his whole head underwater for the pleasure of it. The memory blunted the spikes inside of Anna for a moment.

"What did they want you for, last night?" she asked.

"Them old boys? Bit of company."

"What are you smiling for?"

"I had their leavings for breakfast."

All that work, and they didn't even finish their food. *Sod off back to your laboratory.*

"Hey now," Ted soothed her. "Just a few more days until the fair. Then it's coconut shies and chimney cake 'til it comes out of our noses."

They jumped at the crack of a rifle. Mister Beale was in the fields, screaming about cannons.

Ted jerked his head. "Come on. I'll show you summat."

He took her out into the shed where Mister Gibbon the gardener kept his tools. On the workbench was the black helmet from the carriage.

"Bleeding hell, Ted, you muck around with their things—"

"I polished it."

Ted tried it on. The top of the head was flat on one side, giving him a broken-necked look that troubled her.

"Dabster's alright," he said, taking the horrid thing off. "He's one of us. You should've heard him explain the fair to the other three, like they'd never had a day of fun in their lives. He knows *everything*…"

"No one knows everything."

"He does. Hundreds of years of it. Did you know Cromwell banned the fairs after he killed the king? Said they were pagan. But then the king's son came out of hiding, put Cromwell's head on a spike, and let us have 'em back." Ted grinned. "Remember last year, when you conked out by the fortune teller's tent after all them shandies?"

Anna smiled. Somehow, despite the sunburn, it was a memory she looked back on fondly.

Ted cradled the helmet, nose up, like the head of an enormous crow. "He says it belonged to a spirit."

Anna sighed. It stuck in her craw, city types sniggering about old wives' tales and May Day marriages.

"It's from the story," he insisted. "You know. The blacksmith who jumped into the lake?"

She pushed past him, out of the shed. The sun hit her like a smack from Missus Swinney, and she stopped to rake the sweaty hair from her eyes.

"Dabster collects old tales," Ted went on. "*Verifies* 'em, doesn't he? He found the helmet in Marshbone. Dug it up. The actual one!"

"I've got piss pots to empty."

"Don't be sour. I reckon he'll tip me again. We can split it. How about that? Have a right old time at the fair."

Ted was alright, Anna told herself. For an idiot.

In daylight, the gentlemen weren't as decrepit as they had first seemed. Even Mister Thin, who previously possessed all the vitality of a gibbet full of bones, appeared comparatively well-rested, sucking on his pipe. Anna offered to bring them more shag, but they wouldn't take anything but their own.

Dabster was civil enough.

"My heartfelt thanks for your attentive service last night, my dear. Can't have been comfortable, rushing around in this heat."

He gave Anna such a sympathetic look, it startled her. She imagined herself slapping him, quick as a shot. But her body remained still, like a hare sensing a hunt.

She needed rest.

"What might I fetch for you gentlemen this morning?"

"Come into the light."

The short one waved her over. She supposed his eyes were weak and she stepped closer, bowing slightly so the old ditherer could hear her better.

"There's a good girl. See? Plain as day, on her face."

Dabster held up a hand as if to object. "My dear fellow—"

"Pox." Mister Tall leered into her face. "The chicken pox laid waste to her, see?"

Anna could not move. There, by the window, she knew the constellations of her scars would be at their most visible. All three old men stared as if holding her down, preparing to dissect her. Only Dabster kept his eyes politely averted.

"Is there not some woman's trick to cover them?" asked Mister Thin. "A cream? Or—"

"A mask?" Mister Short interrupted. A laugh burst out of him. "Oh, you mustn't take heed of me, miss. I'm dreadful. A rotter."

Anna rushed out of the taproom. She stopped in the hall to steady her quickened breath.

"She was never going to be a beauty. Nevertheless, a shame."

In the hall mirror, she saw them smiling out after her. As if they awaited the results of an experiment; the final score of the game.

"See? Not difficult," remarked Dabster, pleasantly. "Not difficult at all."

They stayed another night. Anna's dress was heavy with sweat as she catered to their whims. *More matches, more coffee, chop-chop, how about a little smile…*

Ted, however, they adored. There was no detail of his life of drudgery that they did not find supremely fascinating. When Mister Beale saw how delighted they were by his cheery company, he let Ted off one or two small duties to spend more time with them, telling stories and urging them to spend their money. Soon the whole inn was cloaked in the miasma of their peculiar tobacco. The other guests complained, but Mister Beale declared the gentlemen may do as they please.

"Good customers," he said, polishing his rifle.

That evening, hauling in the coal scuttle, Anna almost tripped over Mister Thin, sitting on the back steps with his knees scraping his chin. The bowl of his pipe glowed lazily as the old man stared out at the star fields. The wrinkles on his face seemed shallower. It was remarkable what a short rest could do for a body, Anna had to admit. Not that she had first-hand experience.

"Dinner's served on the hour, sir."

His eyes drifted slowly in her direction. They were the eyes of a sleepwalker, half in dreamland. He must have been at the sherry.

"I took his pulse."

"Sir?"

"A good pulse. He beamed all the while, like a child observing a conjurer's trick. An excellent lad."

He exhaled a serpent of smoke. Anna could taste it, like no tobacco she had ever encountered before. Strong as a housefire.

"We see you, you know," he said. "Eyeing Ted. You country girls, you're all cut from the same oily cloth. Were I a younger man…"

He was cut off by a rattling cough. Anna swept past him into the safety of the inn. His claws snagged a handful of her skirt, which she yanked from him with a curse.

"Not long now, heifer," he wheezed after her. "Let the boy have a fumble, why don't you? Have mercy on the condemned."

Anna dropped into sleep from a great height. She woke before dawn, head aching with thirst and the residue of nagging dreams. Missus Swinney snored in the bed opposite. Any unnecessary second spent awake at the Four Boars Inn was a loss, so Anna rolled over, shuffling on the lumpy mattress to try for another hours' rest.

One of the gentlemen was in bed with her.

Anna screamed. Missus Swinney was up and swearing instantly, but the gentleman lay still, eyes shining in the dark. Dabster, clutching the sheet at his dimpled chin. Anna threw herself backwards, out of bed and onto the floor.

"There's a man!"

Missus Swinney lit her candle. She swept her arm over the empty bed, looked underneath, and checked the door was still locked.

To Anna's shame, she was shaking, pressed up against Missus Swinney's reliable bulk like a bairn at her mother's side.

"A nightmare, you silly cow," said the cook. "Leave off."

Anna lay in bed, rigid as death, breathing second-hand pipe smoke until dawn.

Anna could convince herself Missus Swinney was right, that the man in the bed was nothing more sinister than a nightmare. But she couldn't forget what the thin man had said. *Not long now.* And Ted – 'condemned'. What in God's name could that mean? They loved Ted. Everyone did. When Anna caught sight of herself in the mirror at the top of the stairs, she looked haggard and afraid.

Pigeon.

She delivered the first of the morning hot water to Mister Tall, who wouldn't look her in the eye. The second jug was for the room next to his, that of the odious Mister Thin. When she knocked, there was no answer but the squawking of the jackdaws down the chimneys.

The door was unlocked. Anna bustled inside with the intention of ruining his lie-in. Mister Thin was in bed, eyes closed, the sheets tucked up to the chin. Anna knew that smell: the old man had pissed the bed.

Mister Beale had left for his morning shoot. Anna found Ted in the courtyard.

"Died?" the pot boy whispered. "He was looking better."

They slipped into the deceased's room. Seeing Mister Thin's body a second time, like a bundle of kindling under the sheet, Anna felt her stomach churn.

"Don't fret." Ted took her out into the hall. "I'll get Beale. If you want a moment's peace, make like you're upset and Missus Swinney'll coddle you."

Even now, he was smiling. She wanted to shake him.

"I don't need coddling. I need—"

"The day off, I shouldn't wonder."

It was Dabster, packing tobacco into his pipe. The servants stared, each willing the other to speak first.

"A regular backstairs coalition, you two," Dabster chuckled. "What's afoot?"

"Sir, forgive me, but I think you and I had best leave the lady and speak."

Dabster followed Ted's look to Mister Thin's bedroom door. His smirk faded.

"My dear fellow…"

He took Ted by the elbow, and they went together into the silence of the dead man's room.

As the necessary preparations were organised, Dabster thought it best he and his companions extended their stay.

Ted was his usual bonny self, but Anna knew when he was sore on the inside. Mister Dabster was saddened, and to Ted's mind, that was a shame. The boy took him breakfast in his room, the papers, even a small posy of wild flowers to cheer him. Mister Tall and Mister Short ceased their braying. When they took meals together, they barely said a word.

For Anna, Mister Thin's death meant another room to clean. Grunting with the effort of rolling the carpets for beating, she heard the hum of voices next door, in Dabster's accommodation. To her surprise, she recognised Ted's laugh. Mister Beale had installed a peephole so he could check on newlyweds, and with a minimum of guilt, Anna removed the mirror covering the hole. There was Ted, sitting on the bed. Dabster lounged in his shirtsleeves, smoking with the helmet in his broad lap.

"How well do you know the hills of Marshbone?" Dabster asked.

"Not well, sir."

"Accounts differ on some minor points. Sometime after the Roman exodus and before the coming of the Danes, there was in the county of Hookland a blacksmith. Though he was late in his years, he was strong and straight of limb, and never once ill. His skills were those of a man in his prime, and his manner as merry as a schoolboy's. The envy of the village, this simple craftsman. But this blacksmith was so old, he saw his wife die, his sons, and all his friends, too. In church, he smiled and told the young ones he could never be afraid of death, because he had so many beloved ones waiting for him in Paradise. But when he went home to his lonely forge, the blacksmith would think on the indignities of infirmity, and was afraid. One night, a spirit overheard him – as spirits are known to do – and appeared in the shape of a knight seeking hermitage. 'Blacksmith, will you give me your kindness?'

"The blacksmith, being a good Christian, freely invited the spirit in, and helped remove his suit of armour. But it was like no armour the blacksmith had ever seen. Black as rain-wet coal, and so heavy it ought to have crushed the knight's bones.

"'I barely notice it,' said the knight. 'Not after twelve-hundred years.'

"Now the blacksmith's attention was arrested. When he asked the knight how this could be, he shrugged his shoulders.

"'My wife is a thousand years old,' he said, 'and has nary a wrinkle.'

"The blacksmith declared he would give almost anything to reverse the merciless march of time. He made the knight a meal, apologising for its simplicity, for advancing age brings with it poverty. When dawn came, and it was time for the knight to leave, the knight said the blacksmith must accept the helmet as a gift. For it was a magical thing, and a worthy exchange for the blacksmith's kindness."

"Magical?" Ted said, running his fingertips over the black visor with wonder.

"Cast in a dwarven forge, the helmet had the power to grant a certain invulnerability to the natural decline of life."

"To them what wear it?" Ted sounded worried, no doubt thinking of the morning in the shed when he had so readily tried it on.

Dabster gave a kindly laugh. "Nothing so simple. The knight told the blacksmith, 'You will have youth, your skills, your looks, and your charm. You will find a new wife, and have new children, and they, too, will never grow old so long as you have the helmet and the knowledge of how to use it.'"

Dabster turned the helmet in his hands with a look of fondness, and, as it seemed to Anna, insufferable self-satisfaction. So he'd found a hunk of old iron, had he? A minute's talk with any farmer in the county, and he'd find out that was nothing special. Cannonballs and arrowheads, pottery and bones, all the junk of the ages was down there, waiting its turn to be churned up.

Ted was not so scathing, though his glance was uncertain. "Missus Swinney says good children don't make conversation with spirits. She won't even go to the Puck Fair."

"A most sensible lady," Dabster said. "It is said the blacksmith went mad and threw himself into a lake at the foot of the Bone Hills, helmet and all."

"I reckon if someone offered me eternal youth, I'd make a go of it."

Dabster laughed. "I daresay I would, too."

They quietly enjoyed each other's company. Perhaps Anna didn't need to worry. Ted had a credulous nature, but by this time next week, Dabster would be gone, and Ted would be banging on about the travelling conjurer who could guess the number you were thinking. Anna allowed herself a rueful smile. She didn't know what she had expected.

Dabster put down the helmet.

"Ted, let me be frank. You are a vigorous young man, and I require a manservant. It won't pay well, I'm afraid. Not at first. Probably only double what you earn at the Four Boars, and, of course, your bed and board. There will be a great deal of travel. Perhaps even abroad…"

Anna drew back from the peephole. Ted, leave? In Dabster's room, they were laughing, damn them. Laughing at the thought of abandoning the inn. She quickly replaced the mirror and fled to the kitchen.

When Ted came down, his mind was elsewhere. Anna shovelled coal into the stove. The boy rested his head on the window frame, staring out at the birch trees peeling in the heat. Anna noticed a large, incongruous ring on his finger. An insignia ring, one of those coats of arms fancy old men plastered all over their carriages. The bargain was struck.

"Anna… d'you ever think about packing your bags? Setting off, like?"

It didn't sound possible. Like stepping off a precipice. Anna threw one last scrap of coal into the stove and slammed the door.

"You never asked the blacksmith's side of the bargain. What he had to do," she said. "With the helmet."

The highway shimmered where sky met dirt.

They held Mister Thin's funeral on a Friday, at Saint Mary's at the foot of the hill.

Anna had no intention of going, but Mister Beale said it was a sign of respect to good customers.

Ted, wearing his new ring, stuck to Dabster. When the pot boy offered Anna a small smile at the graveside, she turned away.

Over the churchyard wall and up the hill, tents were being pitched. The colours of the fair shouted loud against the muggy July sky. A pipe organ started up, tootling uncertainly as its owner tested the mechanism.

Riding home on a hay waggon, Anna sat with Missus Swinney, staring out at the tents disappearing in the dust.

The cook wiped her brow with her sleeve. "When my grandmother were small, a little lass went to the Puck Fair and never came back."

"Sad," said Anna.

"They took a net and dredged the village pond. Nothing."

"You ought to come with us," Anna said. "To the fair. Bit of fun'll do you good."

"Her mother was a bad'un," Missus Swinney muttered. The cart bumped over a rock, and they fell into mutual silence.

At the mention of the lonely pond, Anna couldn't help but dwell on Dabster's blacksmith tale. Spirits were not to be meddled with. They were tricksy things, mixing truth with lies to catch good people out on the Devil's account. And stories were just as bad. Stories did naught but make a soul long for what it cannot attain. They weren't kind things.

But that was the blacksmith's side of the bargain, she realised.

His kindness. Which he freely gave away.

Missus Swinney served a funeral supper for which Mister Dabster paid handsomely. Despite the sombre nature of the occasion, Mister Tall and Mister Short looked exceedingly well. Their hair was glossy and their skin clear. The best claret was poured, too heavy a wine for such a stifling night, and as the toasts were made, the two men glanced at each other with an impish excitement which Anna found repulsive.

She kept an eye on Dabster as he beckoned Ted over, waggling his empty pipe. Ted smiled at his new master and went to fetch a box of Lucifers. Anna found herself imagining the inn without his quick, light presence. She realised Dabster frightened her. Not because he was dirty-fingered or because of his greasy companions, but because he had infected the Four Boars with the possibility of escape. Anna could manage hopelessness. Loneliness was something new.

As Ted scurried off, a squat gentleman dining with his wife caught him by the wrist. He yanked the insignia ring from Ted's finger, eliciting a yelp. "Planning to sell it, were you? After parading it under my nose?"

Ted was bewildered. "It's mine, sir."

"Yours! The gall. I've searched for this for days."

By then, Mister Beale had come in with a brace of pheasants over one arm and his gun over the other. "What's amiss?"

"Your urchin ransacked my luggage."

Ted's eyes were white with rising fear. "Mister Dabster gave it me."

Ted turned in appeal to Dabster's table. The three gentlemen supped their soup.

"This is my club ring," the irate guest declared. "I'll write to London for confirmation if you doubt me. And then I shall write to the newspapers – and tell them about the crooked little inn on the highway."

Mister Beale took Ted down the cellar and gave him a leathering. Anna tried to make noise with the cutlery while Hawley the ostler whistled a lacklustre tune. When the crack of Beale's belt ended, the staff made themselves scarce. Ted came up moments later, trembling and red in the face. The offended guest's bill was wiped clean, his ring returned. Dabster ordered three slices of Missus Swinney's gooseberry tart.

Anna found Ted crying by the well.

"I worked hard. I did as I was told. Anna, you know me. I'm no thief."

"There's something wrong."

"Not with Mister Dabster," Ted said, a trifle quickly. The stupidity of it snapped Anna's fraying patience.

"You pigeon. He's rich. He's not going to care about a pot boy. You're here bawling your eyes out – do you think he's in there, worrying about you? The ring was a joke. The job, too. All that lot care about is their tobacco and their cruel tricks. They can go hang."

Anna had no more sympathy left to give. She left him there, weeping by the well.

"You've got a face to curdle milk, lass."

Hawley the ostler was brushing one of the horses. The hay-and-hair smell was a comfort, and Anna had sought it out unconsciously.

Hawley looked over Anna's shoulder, down the long highway where the dusky moon hung, blushing in the heat. He shook his head.

"I've never known Ted to steal."

"First time I've seen him without a smile…" Anna shrugged. She refused to appear upset. "Dabster. What d'you reckon?"

"Not my place to say."

That could only mean something worth hearing. Anna waited while he smoothed the brush down over the horse's long spine.

Hawley sniffed. "You found the dead 'un, is that right?"

"I did," she said.

"How good a look did you get?"

"Nothing good about it."

"I helped the undertakers move him." Hawley eased his fingers through the horse's mane. "He'd bitten his tongue."

"You what?"

"Last time I saw a dead 'un with his tongue between his teeth, it were the war. Not the battlefield, mind. A disagreement over a lady. A corporal took it upon himself to put a pillow over the face of his rival while he dreamed. He hanged for his trouble." Hawley took a final sweep of the horse's flank, and patted it. "I'll be glad when Dabster leaves, is all."

⌇

"There. No hobgoblins. Not even so much as a dobbin."

Missus Swinney made a show of battening the shutters and checking under the beds. The cook was snoring within minutes, but Anna's brain was at war with her weary body. She could cry for want of sleep, but worries fled across her mind, heightening every ache and abrasion from the day's work. The attic bedroom had trapped the day's heat, and Anna felt like a loaf being baked.

With sleep out of reach, Anna slipped from her bed. She imagined how lovely it would feel to creep down to the courtyard and take water from the pump, pouring it over her head and standing in the darkness, dripping and cold. Missus Swinney didn't stir as Anna let herself out. She crept down the stairs, avoiding the creakiest floorboards. A few minutes of relief, then the chance of sleep.

Anna went out across the driveway, barefoot in her nightgown. The coach house was shut up for the night, but moths and midges flocked to the light within. To her dismay, there were men inside, making stilted conversation. Anna was about to give up and return to bed when she realised one of the voices belonged to Dabster. She dared to hope he was preparing to leave, but when she heard the tears in the other voice, her stomach turned. She crept to the door and pressed her face to the crack.

Dabster wiped Ted's tears with his own handkerchief.

"There, now. Character building, eh?"

"On the road together," the boy sniffled, "will we find more helmets? Magic things?"

"Your future will be a miraculous one."

Despite the heat, Anna shivered. *He's apologising. He's a devil, but he's making amends.*

Dabster hung a lantern from a beam. Anna saw the welt across Ted's face; a stripe from Beale's belt, deepening to a bruise. She could say it to herself at last: she hated the inn. She hated the heath it stood on, and the sky above it. She hated the wind in the casements and the spiteful birds with their morning calls – *Another day! Another day!* If the highway led out, Ted should take it, even if it was with Dabster and his odious gentlemen. Even if she couldn't leave with him.

"The pain's not so bad," Ted said.

"No?"

With his grimy fingers, Dabster took the apple of Ted's swollen cheek and pinched. The boy flinched, but Dabster had him again before the pot boy could squirm out of his reach. He pinched and pinched, and when Ted scrambled away, he scratched with his nails.

"Stop it! Stop it, it's… cruel."

Dabster stalked him across the coach house. "The maid was quite correct. You never asked the blacksmith's side of the bargain." He kicked the backs of Ted's thighs where the bruises cut the deepest. Ted shrieked. He fell. He couldn't seem to understand why Dabster was so cheerful. "When the spirit knocked on the blacksmith's door, he asked for his kindness. And he took it. All of it. Do you see? Magic is commerce, Ted. Tit for tat."

Outside, Anna fought with the door. Dabster must have wedged it shut from the inside. In the lamplight she saw Mister Tall and Mister Short step down from Dabster's coach, bearing something heavy draped in cloth. Anna beat at the door, shouted for Ted.

"With the helmet in his possession," Dabster went on, "the blacksmith's kindness drained from him as if from a seeping wound. Finding him cruel and unfeeling, the villagers shunned him. No woman would marry him. He couldn't stomach it, the little acts of spite he was compelled to indulge in, day in, day out, to keep the helmet working its charm. The blacksmith felt doomed to an endless life of loneliness. So he did what any unimaginative fellow would do. He put on the helmet, and he jolly well drowned himself, didn't he?"

Mister Tall and Mister Short removed the cloth from the helmet and set it on its flat head in the straw. They seized Ted by the shoulders and bent him over it, shaking with pain and bewilderment as his tears spattered the iron, trickling down inside the dark helm. He turned his stricken face to Dabster, as if even then he hoped to please him.

"It's interpreted as a moral tale, Ted. But it isn't. It is a set of instructions." Dabster placed his hand on Ted's head, sinking his blackened nails into the boy's scalp. "To extract the necessary ingredients, one must be a little cruel."

Anna's yelling had had awoken Mister Beale. She had never been so happy to see his broad silhouette come bounding out of the dark, rifle in his hands.

"Sir, they've got Ted. They're—"

There was no time to explain. Beale swung the rifle's butt. It was only when Anna lay winded on the floor that she realised she had been struck.

The coach house doors rattled as if battered by a heathland tempest. A flurry of black flakes came rushing through the cracks, peppering Anna's face, pungent and powerful and hot enough to sear her skin.

"Good customers," Beale said, and left her shivering in the dirt.

The gentlemen left before breakfast. They neither wanted nor needed any.

Their pipes were overflowing. Dabster smiled like a toad. Mister Short was scribbling furiously in his scientific pocket book. He had no need for spectacles now.

Mister Beale had the staff line the driveway to see the gentlemen off. As the driver coaxed the horses to the open road, Dabster put his head out of the window. He waved a cheery goodbye. For Anna, bandaged and aching, he reserved a stream of pipe smoke, lingering darkly in the air as he took his leave of the county.

"Devil take you," Anna muttered. She touched the arm of the boy beside her. Ted was subdued, bruised, but whole. "What did they do to you? You can tell me now. They're gone."

Ted watched the coach trundle away. There were tears in his eyes, as if he had just bid farewell to someone most dear.

"Puck fair, soon. All the cinder toffee we can eat. Shandies by the fortune-teller's tent…" He wiped his swollen face, grinning. Then, surprised: "I can't see."

"I'm not forking out for a physician." Mister Beale oiled his rifle, eyes down where they wouldn't accidentally meet Anna's hard glare. "He'll soon get over it. Strong young lad."

Nevertheless, Ted was given a room of his own, for the first time in his life.

"It's this heat," said Missus Swinney. She repeated it to herself over the following three days, as they listened to him up there, bumping into furniture. Ted refused to open his door for meals, silently rejecting Anna's cajoling and Beale's threats. "It's this heat," the cook said when she went to fetch Ted for church and found his bed empty.

As far as the landlord was concerned, the pot boy ran away. To Anna's mind, boys who ran away tended to take their only pair of shoes.

Anna trod the dusty highway. Saint Mary's churchyard lay at the foot of the hill. Under the baking sun the leaves on the stooping trees were parched, their colours muted. Ted's possessions made a meagre bundle. No other souls were awake to see her dig.

"I'd rather be sleeping," she told the mound of earth. Ted's clothes, his boots, and the cocoa tin he hid tips in. With her hands, she had covered them in soil. The wound on her head was leaking again. "I stink. And I never did make it to the fair."

Beale made her work through it. *Short-staffed*, he said. *Blame your fella.*

Over on the hill, the last remaining string of bunting hung motionless in the stifling air. Anna felt her eyes glaze over, half expecting a fairground pipe organ to crank out a mirthless tune.

Right. None of this dawdling. Carpets to beat. Ashes to sweep.

|Don't You Know Mrs Kelly?|

~

I adjust my bonnet, take a breath, and emerge into the lamplight. The bodies in the cheap seats thunder their appreciation with hands and feet and the blessed incense of fag smoke. My *debut*. Climbing up and out and over the glaring precipice, I am overwhelmed by a caustic miasma of spilt beer and the sweat of painted ladies, and I fear I will be sick. My legs beg me to turn tail and run for the wings, but I wouldn't survive it. The master of ceremonies wields his gavel like a sabre.

"Ladies and gennlemun, boys and girls, and assorted livestock: please be upstanding for the comedy stylings of... MISTER – PADDY – SYKES!"

I am too young to have seen the King's Jester, the great Dan Leno, holding court on the stages of London, but I own several records of his most celebrated sketches: the unhelpful waiter, the simpleton at the races, the overexcited shopkeeper. I smile to think of his impish storytelling, his supernatural grasp of character, even in the darkest of times.

At this moment, for all my terror, I couldn't be happier. I drop into a low curtsey as the piano strikes out the opening bars of Leno's gold standard routine. You know the one. The audience are whispering the title in anticipation: 'You Know Mrs Kelly?'

Oh, they'll love this. I've done it every Christmas for the family since I was ten. By the fifth year, mother had found me a bonnet and tatty parasol to parade around in, playing the terrible spinster in front of the mantelpiece, my first stage. Even Grandfather Sykes shuddered with laughter, the old devil. He died some years ago now, before the war.

I have always been told I have a special talent for mimicking Leno's trademark broad, innocent grin. I give the audience a taste of it, sweeping a look over the whole auditorium, up at the private boxes and far into the darkness of the gods where the very poorest sit. Only a few clap, but as any comedian will tell you, they're always suspicious of newcomers. You must take charge.

My pianist strikes out the cue. I sing in the clearest voice I can muster, only wobbling slightly on the high notes.

> *"For twenty-five years I've been doing my bit*
> *To make Jim Johnson a match*
> *I've done everything but ask him point blank*
> *But he won't come up to the scratch.*
> *Of course, I know Jim's very partial to me,*
> *Though never one word has he said.*
> *Though this morning I passed where he's building a house,*
> *And he dropped a large slate on my head."*

Twirling my parasol, I throw a look over my shoulder. "Of course, he did *that* to get my attention."

A gentleman in the front row wheezes. A girl beside him – a rather 'fast' little thing with a red rose in her hair – bares her teeth in a cackle. It's good to make the girls laugh; their beaus always join in. Something to do with not wanting to appear slow on the uptake.

"My Jim's a roofer," I continue, puffed up with pride. "He don't nail the slates *on*, but he stands by and holds the nails for the senior fellows to hammer."

Grandfather Sykes was always tickled by that line. This lot, not so. A titter here and there. I am sweating under my gown. The smoke stings my eyes, and I falter long enough to hear a man's voice ringing out from the upper circle: "You alright down there, mate?"

I'm *dying*, you rotter, I want to shout back, but I haven't the chance. My affronted face in its greasepaint and frame of yellow sausage curls has the audience howling. I have accidentally transformed into every stuck-up pantomime dame Dan Leno ever played. The heckler is shouted down, and I am permitted to continue.

"Of course, I've been married before," I go on with a wistful air. "My first husband, he was a Spaniard. Said he was a count in his own country. He didn't count for much in this. Oh, girls, Spanish counts? Beware of Spanish counterfeits."

The older women cackle. I knew they would. A man in the front row claps heartily – *Crack! Crack! Crack!* – his cigar clamped firmly in his mouth. I feel a thrill, an unfamiliar sense of power, as the tide turns to my advantage. I venture some fancy footwork in my oversized boots, playing the coquette to the delight of all assembled.

"He *told* me that in his own country he was a bullfighter. I found out he worked in a slaughterhouse. And *then* he said that the olive complexion was the colour of his people. The man needed a bath. But you know Jim? Jim's a totally different man. Jim does love me."

The pianist strikes a chord, and I sing with relish:

"My mind's made up,
I'm going to marry Jim,
He'll have to come to church
If he don't, I'll carry him.
For five and twenty years
I've had my eye on Jim
If he won't marry me, then I'll marry him."

Applause! The girl with the rose lets her head drop onto her shoulder. I hope she is enjoying herself, though a small part of me wants to go to the edge of the stage and check that she's not had to many sherries. But the rest of the crowd have warmed to me, so I carry on, into the act's crescendo, the part everyone knows like scripture.

"Jim and I had a row once, and it was all through Missus Kelly. You know Missus Kelly, of course."

I pause, stretching Leno's credulous grin as wide as it will go before letting it drop. "Oh, you must know Missus Kelly. *Everybody* knows Missus Kelly."

The trick of the sketch is to become increasingly shrill with every repetition of 'Kelly' until the word takes on a monstrous, elongated life of its own. My sister Margery would fairly scream laughing at Christmas as I minced around the parlour, stretching and distorting Missus Kelly until she was unrecognisable. For the rest of the year, whenever we overheard the name Kelly, we would catch each other's eye and shake with silent mirth.

"You know Missus Kelly! *You* know – Missus Kelly? *Don't you know Missus Kelly?* Her husband's that little stout man, always at the corner of the street in a greasy waistcoat, keeps a little whatnot shop at the… good life *a-mighty*, don't look so stupid, don't— You must know *Missus Kelly!*"

Up in the boxes, they shriek. I can feel their laughter vibrating up through my feet. Margery had to throw in her job at the munitions factory. Her hands shook. Something in the paint did her damage, I think, but she refused to leave before they forced her. We all have to do our bit. Perhaps this is mine.

"*Don't* you know Missus *Kelly?* Well of course, if you don't, you don't – but I thought you *did*, because oh, what a woman. Perhaps it's just as well you don't know her. She's a mean woman. Greedy. I know for a fact. Her little boy who's got the sore eyes, he came over and told me she had half a dozen oysters, and she ate them in front of the looking glass to make them look twelve. Now, that'll give you an idea what *she's* like."

I see the girl with the rose coming apart at last. Her mouth falls open and hangs there, shaking in the dark. The man beside her throws back his head. His cigar salutes me.

Dan Leno lost his mind in the end. Drink led him a winding path to the asylum. Those recordings I listened to with such reverence were made mere months before his fall, and the note of imperfection carrying through those golden routines adds something, I feel. A thread of poignance running through the laughter. Do you know, in the asylum, he once told a nurse the clock was wrong? And when the nurse assured him it was right, Leno said, "Well, then, what's it doing in here?"

The audience thunders. I must have said all that out loud. I can't recall the next part of the routine, but the challenge is over now. I have taken charge.

The master of ceremonies swings his gavel and brings it down with a crash so loud I lose my footing as I bow. I have to grab the edge of the piano to steady myself. I hear dozens of voices mimicking my own: "*Missus Kellyyyyyy! You must know Missus Kellyyyyyy!*"

In his poor whiskey-pickled heart, Dan Leno longed to be a serious actor. It was part of his breakdown, that need to show the depth of himself, as well as the wit, and never being given the chance. I think a Cockney Hamlet would have been captivating, but the Victorian stage managers disagreed. Dan went to his grave not long after the asylum. To be robbed of one's potential – that is the greatest tragedy there is.

In the wings, the Chinese conjurer up next fingers the long tendrils of his false moustache. I shake my petticoats and take a final bow. The girl with the rose in her hair catches my eye. I see now that the rose has been crushed.

"Missus Kelly!" they are shrieking still, up in the gods. Hard, vicious clapping, the flesh on flesh like gunpowder on a campfire.

The lamps dazzle me. Severe electric light and smoke.

"Wait."

The girl is not a girl.

"Stop."

The rose is something much worse.

I can see them in the front row. Slumped men against slumped women, collapsed in hilarity. I have paralysed them. Still that clapping, rising impossibly as my ears ring. The master of ceremonies should call for order, but I can't see him, let alone hear him. The pianist has gone. Smoke. So much drifting smoke.

I've misjudged the width of the stage. I stumble forward, waving at the people for a second of peace, and before I can draw a breath I am falling. I glimpse the front row as I drop. Men, all of them, still and staring, and when I hit the carpet at their feet I see boots inches thick in mud. The nearest pair are missing their soles, and when I raise my head to view their owner, I see legs wound with puttees green and stinking. My bowels fill with ice. Still they clap. None of them are moving, but that noise is inescapable, and I thrust my hands over my ears.

"Quiet!"

The man in the centre of the row: I know him. My legs have failed me, so I crawl to him and I clutch at his sodden greatcoat.

"Captain Roberts. Captain, do something."

What I had taken for a cigar is a shard of shrapnel. Embedded in his jaw, it bobs at me as he slurs over gritty mouthfuls of liquid.

We have rolled to the bottom of a shell hole the size of a house. I don't remember being thrown down here, but it is raining and the water is collecting around our legs with cold determination. Small incendiary shells fly overhead, screaming like fiery gulls. Captain Roberts is missing half an arm. I can't see it anywhere, but there are other things around us, scattered all over. Roses. Red roses.

"Take charge," Roberts tells me, and dies.

The cacophony breaks Deliah's concentration. She is writing up the day's reports, and the lamplight is hurting her eyes. She folds up her reading glasses and steps out into the hall.

"What is it now?"

"It's Lieutenant Sykes, Matron. He's fallen out of bed."

"Well then, put him back in. You've done it before."

The nurse is trying not to cry. She is fresh out of college, Deliah appreciates, one of the cossetted academics. Every little noise makes them jump, and when the new men arrive from the front, they look at each other so stupidly, not yet capable of masking their thoughts. *More? How can there possibly be—?*

A yell of bewilderment from the lieutenant's room. Another, more stout-hearted nurse strides in to take the new girl's place, and the two women stand in the corridor, listening to her cooing to him, playing mother.

A sniffle snaps Deliah's patience.

"Miss Kelly. Show some restraint."

"I apologise, Matron. I'll manage, it's only…" Kelly wipes her face. "I think he was trying to tell me a joke."

|Bernie|

You will have seen Bernie.

From the window of your Citi2 as it circuits through the Cambridge suburb of Chesterton, Bernie is the old man standing at the bus shelter opposite Abacus Nursery. He is always at the bus shelter. Though your eyes pass over countless people as you rest with your head against the greasy glass, you will have noticed Bernie. Bernie is the old man in the pyjama jacket, and, as usual, the buttons are undone.

Undaunted by the freezing fog of February or the concrete heat of mid-August, Bernie displays his hard, weather-darkened hide to the traffic passing him by. He has remembered to don his slippers today, which is just as well considering the shattered Corona bottle waiting to be dealt with by the council sweepers. For you, on your way to work or on your way home – always one of the two, never anything different – Bernie is a landmark.

The bus never stops for Bernie. Once in a while a new driver will make the mistake of slowing down as he or she approaches the scaly shelter with its covering of fliers for last summer's church fete. As the doors swing open, the new driver will have a moment to take in Bernie's unusual appearance as he stands on the wet concrete: the tough grey hairs of his chest like an old cat's whiskers, the blue pyjama top, vaguely reminiscent of long-abolished institutions, and the rumpled beige safari jacket on top, slipping slightly from one hunched shoulder. In his hand is a Co-Op carrier bag heavy with browning fruit. His pale eyes contrast pleasantly with his outdoorsman's skin as he stares impassively up at the driver.

He says, "Here it comes again".

In these awkward moments, some passengers will glance at Bernie and judge him to be a sixty-five-year-old with a hard life behind him. His elephantine ears give the impression of great age, although no-one has ever concentrated on Bernie long enough to make an accurate estimation. Some will think he is a youngish eighty and hope he remembers how to get home. Bernie may have taken part in the Second World War; the blue pyjama jacket, with a bit of work, could be an RAF blazer. With effort, it might be possible to see Bernie as he may once have been: a young man with a pitchfork in his hand, hefting hay out in Madingley where all those American servicemen were yet to be buried. With a little imagination, Bernie could be inserted into a nineteenth-century novel; the good-natured old fool, maybe, or the vagabond father of the hero, because he does carry a certain dignity, some of the passengers briefly think, in a shabby way.

Most simply think: old.

Bernie never gets on the bus. Irritated and embarrassed, the new driver shuts the doors and remembers not to stop for the silly old git again.

Sometimes, you will notice another person waiting at the shelter alongside Bernie. On Monday mornings, a lone young man in a Sainsbury's uniform. On Thursday evenings, a woman with a toddler in a pram. "Here it comes again," Bernie will say as the bus appears, and the young man will raise eyebrows, wipe nose, check phone. The mother will look steadily ahead while her daughter considers this grandfather figure, this strange, earthy-smelling Father Christmas.

Bernie likes to watch the buses.

He knows that the single-decker Citi2 – your bus – begins its day in the depot halfway between the village of Milton and the council houses of Chesterton. He knows it swings into the Science Park, picking up all the people who had hoped their lives would be more exciting than this – including you, and don't deny it – and then takes them on a circuit up to Addenbrookes hospital, which Bernie, for all his difficulty with old wounds in the cold months, has never been to, at least not under that name. During the journey, the bus will snake across the river Cam and through the pretty centre of town where the famous colleges preside, a splendor of arches and spires and *keep-off-the-grass*. It is the university's eight-hundredth birthday this year. Bernie does not care.

It is the circle that pleases him.

Bernie knows that, after this, your bus will travel over the railway bridge past the old Mill Road workhouse that frightened him, years ago. Then, on towards Cherry Hinton, the dreary parish built on layers of chalk fossils that once attracted men in strange, tall hats. The bus will then return in a wide circle via the noisy epicenter of Drummer Street bus station, through which all the other single- or double-decker public conveyances pass like satellites on their own regular, unchanging beats.

One is coming now. He registers its arrival with a mumble of satisfaction: "Here it comes again."

A Citi2 bus passes Bernie every ten minutes, unless it is late, which it often is, because, as Bernie could tell you, the narrow streets of Cambridge were designed for horses and carts, not fourteen-tonne monsters of steel and glass.

Bernie sometimes finds the buses upsetting. Their unsuitable size, their solidity, fills him with faint, puzzling distress. It will take a long time for them to crumble into nothing, and when they do, they'll be of little use to the earth. Compounds of metal. Hard to digest. Windows and chassis – which is a silly, short-lived modern word, Bernie thinks, like *chardonnay* or *exfactor* – and wheels and handrails and upholstery and petrol made of crushed ancient sea creatures, like whelks and cockles. Bernie doesn't know much about those. His place is on land.

"This was all fields, once," was something he used to say very often, but not any more. Bernie has one of those rich fenland accents, crumbly and dark.

Another ten minutes has gone by, and the bus is passing his stop.

"Here it comes again."

Does he not have a home to go to, the passengers around you wonder? A wife? He is *always* standing at that stop. Whitefriars old folk's home is just a few minutes up the road, on the bus route, in fact, and surely the staff have noticed him loitering? He isn't a tramp. The Guardian readers onboard are aware that the average life expectancy of a homeless man in Britain is forty-seven years. Bernie is not thin or brittle, nor does he appear drunk. Despite his passive watchful look, he is strong, even tough. Alzheimer's, most of the passengers suspect, and are glad when the bus turns the corner.

In the breeze whipped up by the acceleration, Bernie's Co-Op carrier bag rustles like reeds on a riverbank. It is a new invention, a bio-degradeable plastic with the texture of skin that flakes into harmless pieces after eighteen months. Before his current bag, the older plastic variety lasted a few summers, and before that, he had a mesh bag like a fishing net, and before that, he can't recall. At one point, there was something made of hessian. It scratched, he can remember that much.

Bernie is glad his Co-Op bag will not last long before surrendering to decay, but less happy that this usually results in losing his fruit all over the pavement when the bottom finally splits. Bouncing apples and plums roll into the road where he will watch them being squashed into pulp at ten-minute intervals: bus, bus, bus.

No one notices Bernie shuffling to the plum tree in the front garden beside his bus shelter. The plums are small but plentiful, and he likes the gripe they put in his stomach when he eats more than two. It is a regular September sensation. Whoever lives in the house with the tree has never complained at having their fruit stolen. Most of it ends up in the grass; this is a wasteful generation. A garden on the other side of the road boasts a mulberry tree. Bernie avails himself of this every August when the fruit is ripe, and once spied a small polyester Union Jack in the front room, on top of the television. This still makes Bernie chuckle. Plums and mulberries were brought to the British Isles by the Romans, who had a big gold bird, not a flag. No Englishman of good character would uproot a tree and drag it back to his house for amusement. A tree's place is wherever it pleases. They pick a spot and they stick with it. Like Bernie.

Just as the fruit trees are foreign invaders, each year brings a new crop of students to Cambridge. There have almost always been students, but not this kind, flying in from far eastern countries and leaving again with impressive letters after their names. Some of the bus drivers are Polish or Nigerian. Bernie remembers a time when people stayed put. One house, one parish, one church, a room in which to congregate, a space. His roots are tangled in a time when a fellow was a Cambridge man, or a Grantchester man, or a Royston man, and that was what he would remain. The bad old days, the desperate trudge across the shifting glacier, are over.

Catevellauni, Icini, Pict.

Bernie is concerned for a moment. These days he finds nonsense words creeping into his head, like *doodlebug*, and *andalucia*, and *dee-effess-ale*, and he doesn't like it.

It is nearly ten o'clock at night, and soon the last bus will thrum by. It will be empty. Bernie's pyjama jacket is letting in the cold and the old flesh puckers where it hangs loose on the bones. Bernie stands firm. It is only a pause in the timetable; tomorrow at six, the fleet of Citi2s will emerge again from the depot and Bernie's watch will go on.

Bernie's Co-Op bag has a pigeon in it, a wild city pigeon, well dead. Some boys in a small car had come careening around the corner from the chip shop and hit it as it dithered in the road. *Thunk!* Feathers and flapping and dead. Bernie would once have plucked out the feathers and done something useful with the carcass, but ten minutes has passed since the last bus, and he can feel the final one advancing steadily in the distance.

"Here it comes again," he says. The pigeon sits in the bag with the plums for later.

The weather was warm a while ago, and now it is cold. The Polish bus drivers will start to wear their uniform fleeces, and you, as a passenger, will have difficulty seeing out of the windows as the bodies around you perspire in plastic anoraks and thermal vests.

Bernie is unmoved.

"Here it comes again," says Bernie. Bernard. Bernhard. Bearnárd. Berinhard. Bernd.

|Something Borrowed|

~

In the vestry of Frensham Church, in Surrey, on the north side of the chancel, is an extraordinary great kettle or caidron, which the inhabitants say, by tradition, was brought hither by the fairies, time out of mind, from Borough-hill about a mile hence. To this place, if any one went to borrow a yoke of oxen, money, etc., he might have it for a year or longer, so be kept his word to return it.

    —'English Fairy and Other Folk Tales', Edwin Sidney Hartland, 1890.

"It's not a divorce, so why make such a fuss? I never thought much of her."

Dad never voiced his opinions at a time when they might benefit Harry. He had it on good authority that Harry's driving instructor started the day with a can of Stella, but only thought to mention it after Harry had sunk hundreds of pounds into lessons and failed the test twice. Likewise, Dad silently nurtured a low opinion of the head of department who promised to make Harry office manager and then walked away with eighteen grand in siphoned funds. "Any idiot could see he was on the take," Dad said, slyly catching Linda's eye as if she, too, had been aware all along. Poor obtuse Harry, always the last to catch on.

"He's just a funny old man," Linda would say as they drove home. "You're too quick to write people off."

Not quick enough by half, Harry thought. Linda lived in Stevenage now, with Carl, a landscape gardener who once shook Harry's hand at the wedding of one of Linda's friends. He thought Carl was nice. And he was – that was the problem.

So when Dad died, emotions were already serrated. Mostly, Harry wanted to sell the house and be done with it. He told himself he should be glad Linda wasn't around to console him. She never did like to see him cry.

In typical style, Dad left the house to the Gurkhas. Harry stared at the solicitor, mouth slack, as the news sunk in. He could hear the old man now, the smirk sharp in his voice: "Outstanding, the Gurkhas. You know they never draw their knife without it tasting blood?"

Harry swallowed. "I was hoping…" To sell it. To finally get on the slippery property ladder. To move away, somewhere clean, start afresh. The possibilities dissolved as the solicitor stood to usher him out.

"You'll need to prepare the property," she said, tersely polite. She had, of course, seen the photographs.

Even in the sterile, elegant office, Harry could smell the house. After Mum left, Dad's little collections became a hoard, and Harry's offers of help only provoked the old line: "Sort out your own life, why don't you, before whingeing about mine."

It was snowing when he headed out. In the car with him: bleach, scrubbing pads, rubber gloves, and several rolls of black bin bags. If he was lucky, there might be something of value waiting for him under all the detritus. On the passenger seat, rustling as Harry bumped over potholes, was a carrier bag of Carlsberg and a multipack of Doritos. Just the thought of that kitchen made his nose wrinkle. He could call for a takeaway, but that would involve opening the door to a stranger, and the profound shame would hardly be worth a carton of chow mein.

Dad lived on the edge of a village with one shop, a matchbox of a post office, and no bus service. It suited him, but Harry had always felt marooned there. With its worm-eaten floorboards and chugging plumbing, the house was fit for farm labourers, not a young family. Harry's boyhood nightmares fixated on a brown-toothed cowherd haunting the bathroom, fingering a pitchfork. "You're soft," Dad laughed when he came to his parents' room in tears. Other houses in the village had horseshoes nailed above their doors, but Mum wouldn't tolerate such bumpkin superstition, even when Harry begged.

"You think a ghost or a fairy will see a bit of cold iron and just leave? He'll use the back door. Or the chimney. Or the holes where the mice get in."

With her hair hidden under silk scarves, lips thinly painted and never one for kissing, Harry's mum made no effort to exchange pleasantries with the other mothers at the school gates. And why should she, she argued, when they taught their scabby-headed sons to whisper and stare? Dirty Harry. Cowshit Harry who lived in the woods. Fairy.

It was an odd relief to see those woods had been swept away by developers. Nothing had been done with the land, and the hop fields were black and dormant in the winter damp. Dad's dirt drive was hemmed in by a crowd of apple trees dark with fungus, but in the steadily falling snow the scene resembled a charity Christmas card. Almost pretty, until Harry noticed the sodden sofa greeting him under the front window, half alive with weeds.

When the people at the Co-Op Funeral Home had asked him what music his father would like played, Harry had to admit he didn't know.

"A lot of older gentleman pick 'My Way'," said the crisp young woman handling the service, but Harry declined. Dad certainly did have a few regrets, one of which, Harry suspected, was fairly obvious.

He parked up and sat for a moment, holding the wheel, feeling foolish for the need to gather himself. Through the diseased trees he could see a slice of the old village green and was struck by a memory of eating a charred hot dog from a paper napkin while Punch battered Judy.

Only a handful of people turned up at the crematorium, but that was no surprise. Dad's antique dealer acquaintances loitered stiffly, and Harry recognised the retired woman from the village who seemed to make it her business to go to funerals. Harry should have invited Linda; he did fire off a text, as if it were something his ex should know and care about. She sent a card. Her biro condolences carried the sound of her voice, and Harry regretted initiating contact. Needy, that was how it looked.

He unlocked the front door and steeled himself for that stale fog of Dad's pipe tobacco. It took a good shove to push aside the piled newspapers and pizza leaflets, and when he turned sideways and struggled inside, he was greeted by two slouching grandfather clocks and a birdcage full of Yellow Pages. Harry sighed.

Dinky cars. Takeaway cartons. Commemorative plates for royal marriages long concluded. Dad accumulated objects like a Pharaoh preparing for the afterlife. Harry wouldn't be surprised to find mummified courtiers buried amongst all the junk. But it was like Mum said, you can't take it with you. Even the most treasured possession is only on loan.

The plan, Dad always said, was to open an antique shop. A cabinet of wonders. A *bazaar du junk.* "Things people never dreamed they'd see," he'd announce, ever the ringmaster at a threadbare circus. "Things they barely knew they needed."

This was Dad, so it was all hot-aired flummery. Each item – "Carefully curated, thank you very much" – came with a post-it note bearing a tall story. As Harry edged his way into the lounge, crunching over open books and discarded coat hangers, he saw F. Scott Fitzgerald's typewriter (missing a space bar), a jug used by pilgrims on the *Mayflower*, a framed handkerchief dipped in Lord Nelson's blood. *Incredible discovery! A collector's item! Treasure me!* Dad's notes fluttered to the floor when Harry touched them, like withered petals. It would take the entire weekend to landscape a path between each room.

Harry paused at the mantelpiece, crowded with roe deer trophies and teacups leaning in uneasy piles. *Earrings belonging to Catherine the Great, infamous Russian empress and lover of men.*

The paste gems were Mum's. Harry saw her as she was one Christmas when he was a boy, those earrings glinting like cut fruit as she poured herself a Dubonnet. She was beautiful and hard. Not an especially enthusiastic lover of men. Harry held one of the jewels up to his ear, let it swing against his neck. Through the mirror's dust, his flesh was puffy and grey as moist cardboard. Since Linda's departure, he'd rediscovered microwaved ready meals, and his body – never a point of pride – was beginning to soften and fade into middle-age.

Somewhere over the muffling snow, church bells were ringing.

Harry lacked an expert eye, but nothing on the topmost layer of debris seemed valuable. Dominating the coffee table was a huge metal pot on three legs. Harry tapped it, felt its copper heft. Grubby, dented, but if he put it on eBay, someone could plant it up with geraniums.

Dad had taped a post-it to the rim:

The fairy cauldron of Mother Ludlam, witch. Grants pilgrims what they desire, but all loans must be repaid.

Harry felt shock catch in his throat like a hook. Ludlam was Mum's maiden name. The shock turned to rage, uselessly throbbing under his tongue. The old man made no distinction between trash and treasure. Harry often wondered how he had ever come about, what with his parents' coolly cordial relationship. There was a tension to Dad's love, as if Mum were an exotic bird pausing on his windowsill, and indeed, standing side by side, they were hopelessly mismatched; he a dusty pigeon and she something bright, taloned, and aloof. He was loath to make any sudden moves, to crowd her or to startle her, but now she was gone, she was safe to become another collector's item, a scrap of truth taped to a fabrication to lend it body and life.

Harry wondered what it would cost to hire a skip.

Half the bin bags were full within two hours. Coupons never redeemed, teddy bears for children who weren't Harry, broken champagne flutes. The smell of the sepulchre only intensified as he unearthed layer upon layer of ever-surprising debris. The master bedroom contained not one, but seven Singer sewing machine tables. They, at least, would fetch something, but first he needed to hoist them down the stairs, over a sliding glacier of sixties pulp erotica. Wasp-waisted trailer park sirens sneered up at Harry as he descended, feeling like a man on a tightrope. No one knew he was here. He could easily perish under an avalanche of scratched vinyl and Royal Doulton.

Crunching over the shifting landscape, Harry tried to bully the boiler into life. His fingers came away furry with dust. It was going to be a long, cold weekend, he told himself, pausing at the kitchen's greasy window. He stretched, watching the snow's steady descent. He could hear his own breathing, the slowing of his heart. He had forgotten the almost tactile fullness of the night here. A single blot of light suggested the existence of a petrol station a few miles away, but in every other direction, darkness smothered the countryside and Harry with it.

Perhaps Dad had felt the same, all those years living alone. Harry tried to call once a week, but their brief conversations would invariably turn to Harry's unfulfilling temp jobs, his cramped flat, his failure to produce grandchildren. Punching in Dad's number sometimes felt like an act of self-harm. Standing at the top of the stairs, Harry listened to the silence, felt the iron oppression of it. He had contributed to that silence, over the years. If he felt uncomfortable now, it was no less than he deserved.

He bedded down on the old sofa. There was a discoloured dent where Dad preferred to sit, flanked by a man-sized stuffed elephant and an inexplicable tangle of SCART cables. The thought of taking Dad's place unsettled Harry, but it was warmer than the car. If he had a couple of beers, he might fall asleep before his mind had a chance to wander.

The church bells rang out for midnight. Harry's eyes traced the whorls in the stucco ceiling as he picked Dorito grit from his teeth. He should have brought a sleeping bag. Linda always did accuse him of refusing comfort. How could he explain? Therapists talked about filling the void, but not of the void's trickster nature. The sucking darkness wore strange costumes, reacted to inexplicable catalysts. People spoke of babies swapped for changelings, of families tainted by some hereditary melancholy, but the older Harry got the deeper he sank into the understanding that he was simply unsatisfactory. A factory second. The boring fact of his inadequacy touched everyone close to him, spores that spread and repelled.

Mum left on a Tuesday night when the tractors were spreading pig muck for the coming planting season. Harry was thirteen, cross-legged on the hearth carpet, struggling with his trigonometry homework. She served Dad a lamb chop in mint gravy, drained her glass of Dubonnet, and walked out into the night as the church bells called across the fields. Dad was not in the least surprised.

Harry should have brought more beer.

Lying awake wouldn't clear the house. Harry got up, switched on the lamp, and got to work sifting through a stack of flimsy antique periodicals. *Easy ways to do hard things!* proclaimed a copy of *Popular Mechanics*. Harry grimaced. Dad had amassed at least a hundred interwar editions of *Motion Picture* magazine, pretty but worthless. Most of them disintegrated at Harry's touch. The house was damp, but that was the Ghurkhas' problem now.

He lingered over the browning pages, distracted by the cover girls with their sleek bobs and distant, bewitched expressions. Inside, each page was a display of devotion to some beautiful actor or it-girl; breathless descriptions of suit-tails under flashbulbs, of romances ascending and burned out, of daring feats in motorcars and in casinos and on ballroom floors. Suave Americans, mysterious Swedes, dapper Englishmen: with their smooth skin and light step, these idols resembled humans at first glance, but stare too long – as Harry did – and their perfection took on an eerie light, unreachable, closer to the divine. Harry was surprised to taste tears.

TAKE HOME YOUR OWN SILENT STAR!

Harry gazed at the ad for an idle moment, enjoying the naïve illustration of a figure in a top hat dancing with a woman under a streetlamp. *Watch your mailbox, picture fans!* He imagined he was a nineteen-twenties film fanatic with lacquered lips and pencilled brows saving up her pocket money and responding to the ad. What would you get for your money, he wondered? A poster, probably, with a fake autograph. Something to venerate. He tried to bring to mind the names of silent stars. Clark Gable? No, he came later on. What was the woman's name, the one who wanted to be alone?

Yeah, well, solitude might look attractive when it isn't your only option. Not when your girlfriend of twelve years takes off and your father tosses your inheritance to knife-wielding mercenaries.

Dead stars, Harry consoled himself. In a hundred years, everyone is forgotten. All that glitz and worship was nothing but a fairytale played out on celluloid. And celluloid decays.

He flung the magazine over his shoulder, hearing a metallic *thunk* as it landed inside that witches' cauldron. He needed to sleep. There was a bundle of cigarette card albums and lobby cards unsullied by the house's climate. In the morning he could drive out to one of the auction houses and see what they had to say.

Harry could hear the shovel slice into clay even as he lay in bed. The drag of the sack, the *thump* of heavy objects hitting dirt. In summer he liked to have the windows open, to listen to the crickets in the apple trees.

Slice. *Thump.*

Watching *Top of The Pops* that evening, he said nothing as Dad went from room to room, throwing items into the sack. Horseshoes. Nails. The heart-shaped trivet Mum rested the teapot on. Knives.

Now, staring up at his Bronski Beat poster in the dark, he listened with nagging dread to Dad's progress around the garden, digging hole after shallow hole.

"If that's how she wants it," Dad huffed. "By all means."

It wouldn't do any good, Harry thought as sleep tugged at him.

"Leave?" A cascade of metal pouring from the sack. "Fine! Just you try coming back. See how you like it."

Mum said it herself: she would use another door, slide down the chimney, crawl in through a mousehole. She only had to want it.

His mouth was sour with lager and a headache nibbled at the edges of his vision. The hair on his arms, pricked by cold, stood up like a frightened dog's.

Light. He buried his face in the sofa cushions until stale pipe smoke reminded him of his location. In the night, a further metre of snow had descended on the village, casting a harsh, clean radiance through the cobwebbed windows. The diseased apple trees wore deep white skirts, and for a fleeting moment Harry remembered what it was to be a child looking forward to a day of solitary play.

Then he remembered gritters wouldn't come out this far.

"Shit." He forced himself to his feet, wondering if he had the stamina to trudge to the petrol station to buy snow chains for his tyres. Honestly, he was still a little drunk, and his parka was only a cheap thing, thin and useless. If he lost his bearings along the winding country roads, disaster would not be far off.

He could almost hear Dad's *I-told-you-so.*

He was pouring the last crisp crumbs into his mouth when the doorbell rang. Harry jolted, coughed. For a heartbeat, he experienced a rush of that childish faith, a painful leap of hope. *It's her! Dad! Open the—*

It was a man's silhouette through the glass.

By the time Harry had made his laborious way to the door, he mustered a hazy memory of the previous night, of using his phone while finishing a third beer. He must have emailed the auction house. With a rush of nausea, he hoped he hadn't texted Linda.

The porch was like a refrigerator, and Harry hugged himself as he opened the door. The untouched snow dazzled his hungover eyes, and for a moment he could see nothing but the dark outline of a stranger.

His visitor was well over six feet and blessed with a dancer's build. With a lick of black hair swept back from his smooth forehead and the sun glancing off the clean-shaven hollows of his cheeks, the illusion was strikingly monochrome. He was bundled up appropriately in a woollen peacoat and thick sweater, but his slender hands were bare, clasped before him, serenely poised.

Harry blinked. He felt thirteen again, tongue-tied and dumpy. Cowshit Harry who lived in the woods.

He needed to say something.

"Look, I should apologise before you come in. My father was… he was struggling."

The man smiled with absolute grace and understanding. They must get this a lot at auction houses, Harry surmised. Still, he wished they had sent someone less picturesque to shake his Dorito-stained hand.

"Yeah, it's all through here," he went on. Harry never did know how to talk to other men; the best he could do was mimic the business-like semaphore Dad employed to fill the time around plumbers. "Probably nothing. Tea? Coffee?"

The man didn't reply. He strolled past Harry into the chaos of the house, seemingly unconcerned about losing his balance on the lumpen floor. When he reached the coffee table with the copper cauldron, he paused, allowing the tip of his finger to graze the rim with almost deferential delicacy. Copper was sought-after, Harry realised with a glimmer of excitement. He remembered Dad saying the village church had been stripped bare by thieves. Someone could melt the ugly thing down and Harry could finally—

The man offered him a card. Harry was puzzled to see scrolling white script on a background of velvety black:

CALL ME LARS.
FORGIVE MY ENGLISH. I COME FROM DENMARK,
ON THE BANKS OF THE FROSTY FJORDS.

"Oh. Cool." Harry handed back the card and it disappeared into the man's coat. 'Cool'? Who still said 'cool'? At least Harry didn't feel the urge to raise his voice and talk slowly like Dad on holiday in Spain. With a gesture, Harry ushered Lars over to the dining table where Dad had piled most of the cigarette cards – years ago, judging by the thin veneer of cobwebs clinging to the covers. A fresh wave of shame hit Harry, adding to the encroaching tide of nausea and hunger. He was thankful for the house's frigid air.

Lars stared down, the black fan of his lashes almost brushing his cheeks. His long hands rested on the table's edge, as if it were a piano and he was about to play a melancholy song. Harry found himself admiring the man's nails, immaculately manicured and – what was the word? – lacquered. Soft hands, dextrous, yet it was easy to imagine them hauling ropes on a sleek ship skimming across those Danish fjords.

Harry chewed the inside of his cheek.

He wanted to get on with sorting the upstairs rooms. Of course, he couldn't – only his presence was stopping the stranger from pocketing something valuable and pretending it had never been there – but something in Harry's gut urged him to get away, to scuttle off before Lars could… what? Judge him, he supposed. Judging worth was his profession.

The tall Scandinavian was drawn to a set of lobby cards. Wordlessly, he fanned then out. Harry had never heard of the movies they promoted: *The Awful Truth, The Painted Angel.* Despite their age, the colours were surprisingly lurid next to Lars' pale skin. Yellows and magentas rioted with tropical blues and racing greens. *Footlights and Fools, Hearts in Exile.* Laughing girls danced and soulful men pined. To Harry's relief, the lobby cards were untouched by his father's lifestyle. To a collector, they might be more than just quaint.

Lars' handsome face had a faraway look. He reached into his pocket and produced another black card.

LOST. ALL LOST.
REELS MISLAID, DECAYED, DESTROYED.
SO MANY HOURS OF JOY AND WONDER,
GONE FOREVER.

Harry handed the card back, mumbling something polite. The church bells rippled, clean as silver, as Lars turned his big, Max Factor eyes in Harry's direction, holding his gaze for so long Harry was sure he could sense the shadows revolve around the room with the passing hours.

Lars belonged on the cover of *Motion Picture* magazine, tripping through a ballroom with a devoted girl in his arms. He made no sense here in Surrey. Not with that insectile, intimidating grace.

The sound of shattering glass broke Harry from his reverie. He stumbled into the front room to find a length of iron pipe on the windowsill and an icy wind billowing through the curtains, kicking up the magazines and crisp packets strewn about the floor. Under the snow-laden apple trees, he saw the pack of local boys cackling in retreat.

Harry knelt to gather the biggest pieces of glass. Lars glided over, and Harry felt gooseflesh creep down his neck, though whether that was the drop in temperature or the proximity of the wordless stranger, he couldn't say.

"I'm so sorry," Harry babbled, "you came all this way in this weather, and this is how you find me. They used to do it all the time. Bloody kids. Knock-knock-ginger at the witch's house, you know. Dad repaired this window so many times, he—" He broke off, panting. The incessant ringing of the church bells had broken into his head, made him dizzy. And the blood, the blood oozing from his hands. How could he have been so careless?

Lars held out a card between two fingers:

THIS IS NOT A HAPPY HOME.

Lars drifted to the coffee table and draped a long hand on the cauldron's edge. Snowy against the aged metal, it made a faint ringing sound. He slipped his arm inside and produced a sprig of starry apple blossom, as silvery as his own skin. He tucked it behind Harry's ear.

Harry felt the blood drain from his face.

When Mum left, she took no bag, no clothes, no bright paste earrings. Dad's dull acceptance made Harry frantic. She couldn't have just gone, he told himself as he tramped along the sunken roads, checking the hedgerows as if the tangled hawthorn might yield up a clue. Even if she had another, superior family somewhere, even if she planned to take one of her silk scarves and hang herself in the woods, she couldn't just vanish. People were never simply spirited away, he argued, to Dad, to his teachers, to the mothers outside the school gates, to Linda, and though all those people nodded their heads, their eyes were unconvinced. Mum's presence in his life was temporary, on loan. Harry seemed to be the last to realise, as ever.

"What are you… What are you offering?"

ONLY WHAT YOU NEED.

"How do you… know what I…" Words were beyond him. Little by little, they left him, as if replaced by mouthfuls of snow. To make a sound now, with the cold wind sneaking noiselessly through the broken window, seemed gauche, offensive. Lars with his elegance and beauty was so perfectly silent. The hand that secured the apple blossom turned slightly as he retracted it, showing its wafer thinness, a flawless celluloid dream.

How easy to love someone wordless and distant.

How ravenous he was to be loved in return.

Harry stood, crunching glass and junk. He had one of Dad's post-it notes and held it up for Lars to read:

Treasure me.

Lars blinked, slow, feline. He drew a card.

MY DEAR, YOU KNOW HOW THIS WORKS.

Harry shrugged, lips tight in a weary smile. The church bells called out over the frozen hedgerows, a toneless plea: *Come-home, come-home.* He knew well enough by now.

|Nine|

~

She almost didn't make it. Breech birth, came into the world a fearful blue, and I, half dead myself: "Why isn't she crying? Why isn't she crying?"

It took two minutes and a shot of epinephrine to save her. I held her for the first time, tracing a fingertip over her feathery ginger brows. Some babies are hairier than others – the books all said that. She was incredible. And alive.

She was eighteen months when I turned my back on the bath. The phone was ringing. I was waiting to hear back about a job. It was only a moment. Half a minute. Stupid. Stupid.

The paramedics declared it a miracle. "A water baby," said one of them, soothing me through the shuddering aftermath. "Look at those webbed toes."

"She doesn't—" I protested, but my baby's wrinkled foot was splayed in the man's hand, each pale toe linked with a garland of translucent skin.

I quit breastfeeding as soon as I could. She was a biter. And she only got hairier, my little ginger girl, bounding around with the others at preschool, afraid of nothing.

Her teacher said she snatched the bee clean out of the air. I carry an EpiPen now. I find myself compulsively touching it, as if there's a war on and I need my gun at my side, you know? We lost her heartbeat for a full minute. The doctors assured us it wasn't long enough to damage the brain, but sitting at her bedside, I had my doubts.

The scar? Yes, it was my fault: I moved my chair as she slept, and the noise startled her. Her eyes snapped open as she lashed out, webbed little fingers twisted into claws.

"Mummy," she mumbled, bewildered by sleep. She clutched at my arm where the needle-thin gouges beaded with blood.

"It's alright," I said. And she kissed it better with her sandpaper tongue.

|The Subtle Feast|

I was born with the cord tight around my throat, blue in the lips and silent. Midwives talk of babies who slip from the womb with the caul stretched thin over their eyes, granting them fluency in the language of omens and portents. We don't entertain such ideas where I'm from, but as the judge bowed his head for the Black Cap, my urge was to laugh. I had long known that if I, Amos Hynde, were to die, it would be at the end of a rope, by Edward's side.

Enter the world dead, leave it kicking. I turned to Edward in the dock, watched his black eyes pass over the assembled court like none of them were fit to buff his boots. Years spent by his side, tending to his peculiar wants, protecting him from them as best I could, and for what? Looking back at our time spent together, I could barely grasp it. Snatched memories stuffed into my pockets along with jewellery pilfered at gunpoint. I always had struggled to recall all but the most potent recollections.

"It's alright, Aim," Edward said as we were bundled down into the dripping cells. "It's for the best."

And the bailiffs glanced at each other so queerly.

A hare gambols across the field. Amber eyes, crackling with moon-craters, it fears nothing and knows plenty. Amos knows such fancies are superstition, but he feels a chill down his neck all the same, standing on the roadside with his collar high about his cold ears, watching these animals with their supernatural speed and their wise, desperate faces.

It's something to do, the endless walking; something other than embroidery or cheesemaking. Hares. Fields. The slate spire of Saint Peter's. Father's sheep bumbling beneath like balls of cotton. Amos is never fully here. At the dinner table, saying grace with his parents and two brothers, he feels a lightness in his bones, as if it's only the weight of the mutton and potatoes inside of him that stops him fluttering away like a piece of cheesecloth in the wind.

"We've the funds to rent a townhouse in London," Father says one evening, his smile shyly proud on his craggy face as he spoons at his stew. "Imagine that. A bolthole, a place to do business. Mary, you could travel down with us, see the latest fashions. John and Samuel can hold the fort."

London. The word touches Amos like a leech underwater. A place he's never seen, nor knows the size or shape of. London, testing his skin for an inroad. A tickling underfoot that frightens him a little, yet excites him.

He nearly feels a true emotion for the first time in months.

I was wandering the shore of the Thames when I first encountered Edward. A foggy evening, clinging cold to my bare throat. Hunger gnawed me hollow. I had no bed for the night and no coin for a meal; only my meanderings kept the blood pumping. I must have been robbed – I cannot recall. Father always warned me about the dangers of the city, how a young man with an open face is a target for all sorts of villainy. I never listened to my father. He was a business-minded man, his head stuffed with wool, and despite his gentle nature we rarely saw eye-to-eye. He had hopes for me that were impossible to meet.

And then there was Edward. A motionless shape in the fog, slender as a reed, though few things grew in the brackish filth where the barges bobbed between the drooling sewer mouths. So like pipe smoke was the night air, I couldn't tell if this stranger was staring out at the waters or back at me. This was Wapping. They hanged buccaneers here and left them to dangle; I could remember that much. If I believed in restless spirits, I would surely have mistaken him for one.

He bent down, as if noticing something near his feet. I heard the mud sucking at his boots. If he wasn't careful, he would lose them. I had heard stories of children drowning in the mud, of careless drunks found tangled in fishing nets like bloated river monsters.

I called out: "Sir, the mud is treacherous."

"Mind your business," came his answer. A voice dark and sweet, like sailors' rum.

"Can't," I said, stepping closer until my boots touched the worm-eaten slats of the jetty between us. Again, I called to him, keeping my tone light: "What's that you've found?"

His head turned, long hair flying. "A ring."

I was surprised he answered me so affably; candid and animated, like a child. "Well, then," I went on. "Can't sell it if you drown."

I saw it in the lights of a passing barge: he slipped the ring onto his finger. After a lingering look at the boats bobbing in the scum, he trudged with difficulty up the bank and faced me. We were the same age, I realised, only he was tall and well-formed where I resembled an ale cask. My mother often spoke wistfully of young brides in the village blessed by beautiful babies, implying that she herself was cursed. This young stranger, with his crinkled black hair and round, mobile eyes, was blessed in looks, alright. But he carried himself like a man condemned.

He studied my face, as if trying to place me within some dim memory. Son of a prosperous man though I am, I was dressed like any other youth seeking his way in the city. He would later tell me I reminded him of a hound; bright-eyed and eager, pleased with myself to have captured such vermin as he.

"Amos Hynde," I offered.

My hand remained at my side, but he snatched it up, pumping it with muddy enthusiasm. "Edward Rooke. When I'm hungry, I get the most morbid fancies. Supper? I know a cheap place."

You would have followed him too.

He walked me to a crooked little inn behind the boat builder's yard. We shared a bowl of gristly mutton stew there, and too much watered-down wine.

With the firelight catching in his overlong hair, he supped with one eye on the door, restless even then, before we'd begun our strange partnership. His glance flashed at me, looking me over in greedy draughts. We were equal in our shabbiness – I couldn't recall when I had last had the chance to bathe and launder my clothes – but Edward, furtive though he was, possessed a hauteur that left me in awe.

"It's a gesture of comradeship to share food," he said, chewing. "Trust and all that."

"I'm happy to be eating at all," I replied.

"Are you? I forget more often than not. I need a wife. Someone to nag me." As he used his knife to pick at a knot of gristle between his teeth, he admired the ring he found in the mud. "Glad I didn't come away empty-handed."

He held out his hand as if inviting me to kiss it. A nice little trinket – gold, with a skull carved into the band, wide and flat like an autumn gourd. A lady's mourning band, lost in the river's black silt.

"I'll keep it," he said, adding cheerfully: "I was planning to drown myself."

"I know."

And I did, that's the thing. A *thump-thump-thump* in the hollow parts of myself spoke of danger and then there Edward was, on the precipice.

He regarded me. "Amos Hynde… What brings you to the city, Aim?"

Wanderlust. Pride. I'd wanted to see real streets, the bustle of industry, like the bargemen around us now, laughing between gulps of ale. No, these were lies. I wished to become new.

"Nothing in particular," I said. "My family are in wool, up east."

"How boring."

I liked his ability to cut right to the heart of things. We smiled at each other.

He nodded at my hand, cradling my cup. "What happened there?"

My own ring finger on the right hand was little more than a stump. An old wound, well healed, and barely noticeable to myself except when I attempted to handle a quill.

When I didn't answer, Edward brought the knife to his gleaming teeth and gave it a teasing lick. "Sheep bite it off?"

John finds Amos at the millpond. The turbines spray cool droplets with every turn. Horace, the miller's donkey, gives the occasional docile haw as he turns the millstone inside. The grass is crisp in the summer sun, and the girls of the parish have gathered in the meadow, making corn dollies for the children. When they saw Amos trudging up the lane, they laughed at the acid commentary of Hannah Catchpole, the miller's daughter, always ready with a cutting remark. Amos kept his gaze averted.

A hare keeps him from total solitude. It sits on the far side of the pond, long paws tucked catlike, resolutely paying Amos no attention. It feels respectful, somehow, this shared disinterest, and Amos offers mutual deference by enjoying the shade in silence.

His brother, of course, has to intrude.

"Are you not making dollies?" John asks. He stands in the sunbeam, picking whiskers of corn from his coat.

"Don't make me laugh."

"Father received a letter. The house in London – the lease is his. I'll be travelling down with him to investigate the cloth markets. I'm sure he'll invite you and mother, when the place needs titivating and such…" John shields his eyes from the sun. "Is that a rabbit?"

He scoops up a stone from the pond's edge.

Amos says, "Don't."

"They eat the crops."

"They have to eat something."

John throws the stone. It lands wide, bouncing down the bank and disappearing into the pond's rim of algae with a plop. *The hare is unbothered.*

"It's sick, probably," John says. "They go blind."

He hurls another stone. It strikes the hare in the chest with a hollow sound.

Amos sits up. "John!"

The hare still doesn't flee. Its great ears flatten behind its skull, giving the face a gaunt, old-mannish appearance Amos finds momentarily appalling. He is struck by the sudden impression that John would stone him, too, if it were permitted. The village girls would take their turn, no doubt, giggling as pebbles pitted his cheek, specked with the black whiskers Hannah Catchpole calls his bumfluff.

Just then, there is a commotion from the mill. Horace the donkey is making a racket, and a man's cry follows, rabbit-shrill.

John gets to the mill first. He tries to shield Amos from the scene inside, but Amos sees enough from under John's arm. Catchpole the miller is bent double, pinned between the rolling millstones. His shoulder is hinged at an uncanny angle. The flour has turned to scarlet grit, trampled by Horace. Normally such a placid beast, the donkey rears with white-eyed panic, refusing to back up and release the stone from Catchpole's crushed arm.

John gives Amos a shove. "Run for the physician."

And a priest, *Amos does not add. But he runs all the same. As he takes off in the direction of the village, he notices the hare still loiters beside the pond, cleaning its whiskers.*

Our acquaintance was barely two weeks old when Edward and I committed the first of our robberies. "Beginner's luck?" I whispered, cramming candlesticks into a sack, but Edward was no novice housebreaker. He had watched the little house by the highway for some time and knew there was one old man inside, hard of hearing, and his sole maid was in love with the boy who sharpens the knives. She sneaked out for trysts when the master was abed and wasn't too cautious about locking the back door.

When Edward first suggested burglary – tossing the possibility at me like a plaything – I'd laughed, but he waited in quiet patience for me to come around to his will. He was accustomed to getting his own way, even then. I was incredulous enough, but penniless, and that night I'd followed him through the house's dark passages, hardly daring to breathe as the old man snored and farted in his chamber. We made off with a small fortune in silverware that night. The maid, I can only imagine, was dismissed. Later, I felt a twinge of guilt to think of it, holed up with Edward in our rented room decorated with river mud and the footprints of rats. But Edward's shining eyes as the fence handed over our ill-gotten gains banished all feelings of sympathy to the wind. Edward told me I brought him good luck. I basked in that praise as he lay twirling his hair around his finger, an undertaker's ribbon.

"Another tomorrow, then move on, I think. Bristol, perhaps. I hate the air here. You'll come, won't you, Aim?" He propped himself up on an elbow, beseeching me with his eyes, all bootblack and tragedy. "You must."

Once, I had feared my life contained no meaning. Now, it was my task to keep Edward Rooke content. This I knew in my bones.

There's a hammering at the door that wakes the whole household. John and Samuel race down the stairs in their nightshirts. Father is next, struggling into his banyan. Lastly, Amos escorts Mother to the panelled hall. Catchpole the miller was laid to rest early last week, but ever since the funeral Mother has been restless, sensitive to the rumours passing amongst the goodwives of the village. One cannot blame an animal for taking fright and causing an accident. One can, however, speculate on the cause of the shock, particularly when Catchpole – ignoring the urgings of the parish reverend – had refused to put a name to it.

John is already unlocking the door. "Someone needs help," he says, though how he can know that is a mystery to Amos. The thumping fills the hall.

Mother hangs back, fearful of robbers. "At this hour?"

Father, with poker in hand, herds John away. "Who goes there?" he calls out, and for a moment the noise ceases. "This is a private house."

The Hyndes listen out, holding their breath. Just as Father looks about to speak, the racket resumes with vigour, as if the visitor is pounding with both fists and a boot.

Samuel, the most prudent of Amos' brothers, rushes to the parlour where there is a clear view to the front door. He presses his face to the glass window there.

"They've hidden themselves," he calls to us, though this can't be true. The hammering on the door is insistent as ever. Samuel's eyes must be dim with sleep.

"Enough," says Father. Poker raised and ready, he gestures a count of three, and when he hauls open the heavy door as quick as his stiff old back will allow, the family are met with an unexpected sight.

Amos urges Mother back to the stairs. "Who is it?" she asks, her voice high with dread.

Father lowers the poker. Amos can't see past him into the dark garden; his brothers, taller than him, jostle to peer over Father's shoulder.

But the boys are laughing with relief. Father gestures with his chin. "Don't be afraid, my dear. Look at him. Bold as brass."

Around the well, Mother's daffodils sway in the night breeze. The moon is nothing more than a silvery suggestion behind the cloudbank. On the front step, where Amos kicks the mud off his boots after walking in the fields, there sits a hare.

"Go on, young lass," Father tells it, mock stern now the threat has passed. "Leave us to our rest."

The hare regards them with unblinking amber eyes. Scruffy and long-limbed, it is no different to any other creature of the hedgerows, and yet there is a cool intelligence in the pinched face that Amos is unsure how to meet. He experiences a peculiar impulse to sketch a small bow, the way one must when presented with a lady.

"Witchcraft," Mother mutters. They scoff at her, the three sons. There are Papist symbols carved about the house by former occupants: wheels and aves on beams and around the fireplaces. Protection from the advances of evil.

Mother unwisely refuses to have them scrubbed away, half-believing in their efficacy despite their idolatrous origins. The hare knows nothing of these protections. It watches the Hyndes without fear, even when Father waves the poker.

Amos steps out. "Let me."

We made for Bristol the following week, having fenced the old man's silverware. We resisted the urge to spend the proceeds on sleek new clothes that might arouse suspicion, though I did pine for a pair of the beautiful riding boots I saw on every smart young man in the capital. Edward couldn't resist a knife he noticed in a pawnbroker's window. Carved into the ivory handle, the words *I bite*.

Bristol was elbow-to-elbow with people, and rich as butter. We spent the summer there, hopping from inn to inn and helping ourselves to the customers' pockets as Edward pleased. Experiencing the city with Edward was thrill enough for me: coffee houses and confectioners and tobacconists and sailors, everywhere sailors, rowdy and roving. I feared them instinctively, being small and shabby – a natural target for brawlers who didn't fancy a challenge – but Edward kept his knife close to his right hand. No one would harm us, he said. He was protected.

"I must have been five, perhaps six," he told me one night over a third mug of ale. "My mother took me to a neighbour's house. The old woman there needed help to bathe, so my mother left me in the parlour while she did her duty – always applying some poultice or other, she was. I amused myself with the neighbour's trinkets. She had a basket of fir cones for kindling, and there was an old cat who wanted nothing to do with me. But a box beside the hearth caught my eye, the sort of box a boy might find a nice little knife in, you know. I opened it. I was disappointed. Nothing interesting inside, only a black leathery thing like an old root. I was examining it when Mother caught me; gave me a good smack. 'Not for you,' she said and snapped that box shut like there was rat poison inside."

"What was it?" I asked.

Edward licked the foam from his lips. "Take the hand of a hanged man while he still swings at the crossroads. Pickle it. A woman properly trained will know how to do the rest."

I didn't hide my revulsion. "The rest of what?"

"The Hand of Glory grants invisibility to a thief. It's a sought-after talisman in our circles, Aim. My old neighbour made one for her husband and he had a great career as a pinch-purse until the palsy took him. She taught my mother the trick of it, though she never used it. Couldn't quite stomach the corpsey business. She was more about candles and pennyroyal tea."

I was a little drunk, and my thoughts spilled across the table. "Your mother dabbled in witchery?"

Edward grinned at my horror. "Dabbled? Oh no, the full *maleficium* went on in our house. Love charms, getting rid of warts, solving unwed girls' problems, all that. If she'd been born a little earlier, I'm sure the witch finders would have pricked her. She always said she did it to provide for me. I found it stifling. Silly, really. She was only being a mother, in her way. But I had to leave, Aim. You know how it is with apron strings."

I supposed I could recall my mother well enough, though now, when I put my mind to it, I could only envision the worry she wore like a shawl tight around her shoulders. I upset her, I knew I did. The very sight of me, misshapen and swarthy beside lovely John and Samuel, her strong sons.

Edward reached across the sticky inn table and squeezed my hand. "I'm bored," he said. "What say you and I find some mischief?"

With his family crowding at his back, Amos approaches the hare with cautious steps. The wild thing stares at him, coolly perceptive, though Amos knows he is projecting his own human sensibilities onto the animal. Mother is right, though — there is something witchy about the hare. Sent, perhaps, by one of the village's lonely crones, to frighten or to warn. Who knows why witches do what they do? Boredom, perhaps, a longing for life to be more than drudgery in draughty rooms. Amos can understand that much. And yet the hare's ragged fur is enticingly soft. It feels like a gift, dropped here in the middle of the night, to cling to and snuggle like a child with a poppet.

He slowly squats, puts out his hand.

A breeze steals through the garden, and the daffodils bow in unison.

Pain tears through Amos. He clutches his burning finger to his chest, but not before he sees the white slice of bone. Blood, hot, soaks through his nightshirt, and he topples backwards into the hall. It's bitten him, far worse than he would think possible. It's as if the hare has shears for teeth.

"Unnatural thing," Father cries, and before Amos can shield his face, John is there, bringing down the iron poker onto the hare's head. Amos doesn't know whose blood is whose, only that it is hot and holy on his lips.

People reacted to Edward, I learned, as the summer grew old. He was a swaggering pouch of gunpowder. People either fell for him in an instant or drew swords. Edward was happy enough to brawl, but he viewed adoration as merely his due and kept women at arm's length. On the rare occasion he did pick a paramour, we went to her together. Edward's wiry frame with its white tigerskin scars set a fire in me that felt like pride. The girls ignored me, scrunched up in the corner like a chaperone. Few people paid me attention, eclipsed by Edward's radiance. A small price to pay to be the first to see him in the morning and the last to watch over him at night.

But Edward's power needed fuel. Any time he wasn't the centre of attention, he crumpled. Ordinary – anything but that. He had to be the most admired, the source of light in any given room. More than once I saw him reduced to bitter tears by some meaningless slight, retreating to whatever flea-ridden mattress we'd rented for hours of silent brooding. I learned the knack of coaxing him back to life with praise and cheap thrills. *That fellow isn't watching his purse*, or *I bet we could clear out that shop one night.* And it worked, by God, though I felt those little sins hot within my chest, like burning chestnuts. Risks taken too lightly. I wondered how it would feel to be branded, or to be locked in the stocks. How it would feel to see Edward treated thus.

He would drift to some new diversion. I held fast to this conviction, though it felt more like superstition with every passing day.

One muggy August night, the press gang came to town. All the single men dropped their drinks and hid. Some pretended to be married, bribing publican's widows to hang on their arms, or skipped town completely, walking all night off-road so not to be caught and dragged back to ships bound for the Caribbean. We all knew the stories: anyone slowed by drink, or without a bed for the night – or even those who had – were snatched away, marched through the street, shivering and bewildered, towards the docks. Edward knew this dance. As soon as the men appeared, stalking down the street with their cudgels, he hauled me into the inn where we shared a room, half-dragging me up into the attic, and ordered me to hide behind some linen chests.

"What about you?" I whispered.

He tossed back his hair, scraping it into a ponytail. "Score to settle."

"You know these men?"

"They're not taking us, Aim." He paused, and when he blinked I saw the salt water brimming beneath the lashes. "Not again."

I lay in the attic for what felt like all night. What if he didn't come back? What would life be worth without him?

When he returned, he had with him an unfamiliar ditty bag slung over one shoulder. A bruise shone around one eye.

"What happened?" I asked.

"We're leaving."

"You're hurt."

"Stop mithering and get a move on."

Later, miles away, holed up in a stable with a loose door, I watched him scrubbing dried blood from his knife hand, the golden skull glinting there like an oath. He slept as I kept watch, and when we rose before dawn, he said nothing of the preceding night.

"Aim, I've had a thought…" he said, picking blackberries from the hedgerow for breakfast. "Do you shoot?"

Coaches, rattling along the highway. I'd lain awake listening to them all night. I saw his thoughts and my gut turned with dread.

Two weeks pass in sweats and sleepless nights. Amos is too tired to help Mother about the house, yet too sore to rest. The smell of dinner makes his brow prickle with nausea, even the fresh knots of bread Father brings home, and when he squats over the chamber pot his urine comes dark and pungent like bad ale.

"You look like a toad," John tells him, and Samuel agrees, though he musters a degree of sympathy.

"Cast your mind to wholesome things. Think of the new London house," he suggests. "Father says you can pick the drapes."

Amos' finger throbs and oozes. The thought of loitering in a draper's shop and making choosy sounds over bolts of damask makes his guts lurch. When the sun goes down, he stands at his open window in the blessed cool and looks out over the fields, stubbly after the harvest, and he wonders what might lay beyond them, mile after dark mile through the woods and the fallow. And where are the hares tonight? Tucked up in their solitary ditches, amber eyes squeezed shut? Or do they convene like old women in the secret places of the earth, making their pacts and sowing their schemes? If Amos could start his life over, say the right words and scratch the right sigils…

A cry from behind him startles him from his reverie. Mother is calling for aid. Amos is on his side, chin wet and slack against the rush mat. He can smell his own body down here, as if he is removed from himself, delivered of it: a miasma of sweat and sweet corruption.

Robbing coaches became Edward's favourite intoxicant.

We averaged one coach a week. The papers printed pictures of our deeds, horrid cartoons depicting Edward as a fiend with a corona of hair like a halo of smoke. They ignored my existence altogether. My dumpy body didn't lend itself to the high romance of crime.

HIGHWAYMAN: Edward thrilled at the word. It was shockingly easy, running down slow, trundling coaches driven by nervous men who'd never raised a fist in anger. Edward stopped them practically singlehanded. I stood by, the wordless accomplice, watching the desolate stretch of road with my pistol held aloft as if I knew how to use it. Women wept as Edward tore away their jewellery, sometimes putting it on over his mask and gloves, preening for his captive audience. Their husbands vowed we'd hang, and Edward gave that laugh of his, lovely devil that he was, and we'd disappear into the woods like ghosts.

I had hoped it would be enough.

One night, I was foolish enough to say so.

Edward was silent the whole ride back. At our rented room, he waited for me to turn the key in the lock before crushing me face-first into the door.

"Who are you?"

He forced me to my knees. There was something slack about his face, like a coney hanging in a poacher's hut. Before I could stutter out a response, he slid the pistol's barrel over my tongue. It was cold and tasted of soot. With my eyes I pleaded with him to recognise me as his friend, his Aim.

"Tell me!" He sprayed my face with spittle.

If his finger slipped, the death would be a bad one, blowing out the back of my throat to leave me choking on my own fluid. He wouldn't, not deliberately, but when he tumbled into one of his dark moods, there was no telling what he might regret later. *I bite*, said the knife in his belt. He was honest, my Edward. Like a gut wound.

"I ought to slit you stem to stern," came his shaking voice. "See what's inside."

He drew back, wiped the spit-wet gun on his breeches. He didn't meet my eyes as he reset the hammer, twisting the skull ring around his bony finger as if it might bring him back to God's miserable earth.

"We could give this up," I said, remaining on my knees. "Take our money and go somewhere far away, buy a little farm, raise sheep. I know how. We'd be happy. And safe."

And Edward fell upon the bed, disassembled there, hair falling over his dazed eyes. "I'd be bored. And I'd turn on you for it."

You can, I thought. *If you need to. Better that way.*

I licked the gunpowder from my teeth as I watched him drift into a fitful sleep. It was my task, after all, to keep him content.

The physician is summoned as Amos sweats and tosses in his bed. It must come off, the finger. The bite is ragged, seeping hot. Nothing for it. "It will be quick," Father promises, but doses him up all the same, with brandy and poppy and a lashing of prayer.

It comes like a second bite, a hard press of cold teeth and a burn that throbs and leaps with his heartbeat. He moans and struggles, but there are hands holding him down, and John's hot breath in his ear, unconvincingly jovial: "It's just a finger. You have others."

As Amos sleeps, he dreams of his mother speaking in a low voice.

"Nineteen years old and no courses. She used to pluck her chin every day, but now she lets the hairs grow. She's well-formed enough, but her voice is like a boy's…"

The blankets shift around him like dunes, and he kicks weakly, a thumpa-thumpa *drum of danger in his ears. The air is ice-sharp against his skin, and the strange hands on his thighs drag their calluses. He feels tight, swollen, like a ram rotting in the sun.*

"When she was born, the midwives had to rub her back to life like a pup. Not a sound out of her. Could the ordeal have… damaged her somehow?"

Amos' lips draw back from his teeth. Something, stirring on the distant surface of his consciousness, is wrong.
"We may yet have to take the arm," a man says. "I'm sorry."

The stack of pamphlets fluttered in the breeze outside the printmaker's shop. Edward had overheard a tipsy man in a tavern claim the owner kept obscene French works in a hidden compartment in the back room, along with a cash box and the details of his most discerning collectors. It was a different speed to highway robbery, but the parish constables had their eyes on the roads; it was almost time to move on. Edward couldn't resist novelty. Plus, there were posters of him in the window, a masked man festooned in bracelets and diadems. I should have worried: I would know those eyes anywhere. One admiring glance could hang us both.

I leafed through the pamphlets as Edward sauntered around, hands in pockets, evaluating the premises. Religious tracts were unusual where I came from. After the civil war, my father said, people were wary of zealotry. I leafed through the pages, my eye falling upon a line by some long-dead Puritan: "A good name is a thread tied about the finger, to make us mindful of the errand we came into the world to do for our master."

Edward glanced over my shoulder. "What does your name mean, Aim?"

Something prickled in my throat. I shrugged, willing it to pass. "'Carried by God', I believe."

"Carried." He considered this. "Don't make that face. Are you surprised I can read? I learned at my mother's knee. Not much, mind you: I was ten when I ran to the Navy. Thought the life of a powder monkey was one worth living." He kicked at a stone, sent it flying. "Idiot."

He linked his arm through mine. The *thumpa-thumpa* of my heart was sweet and painful. He rarely opened himself to anyone; these crumbs of his past were a banquet to me.

"What was she like, your mother?" I asked. "When she wasn't casting spells."

Edward took a breath and blew it out through puffed cheeks. "Sad. She had a great deal of cats. I was the only one of her children who lived. It turned her brain, I think. She had a habit of wafting candles around the house, calling it 'the subtle feast', feeding the familiars and the departed, you know."

"Have you eaten today?"

"Ah." He met my eye with a grin. "My wife didn't remind me."

"Shut up, you great lobcock." As I turned my flushed face, I saw the shopkeeper at the counter watching us, his expression one of hushed concern. Time to go. I gave Edward's boot a gentle kick.

"Come on, then," he said, directing a saucy look over his shoulder. "There's nothing of value here."

When he wakes, his arm is still attached to his trunk. Both of them, when he checks. And the surgeon has spared his legs, right and left, and each cold foot, and the thatch of hair on his head, and—

Eyes open. He's out in the fields in the shadow of St Peter's. He lies on his back inside a hard furrow, and the shock brings a wave of nausea he covers his mouth to fight. A viscous wetness cools between his legs. He tries to sit up, but there's a sucking, dragging sensation in his guts that makes him fall back and cry out for his mother. Mother has gone to London without him, perhaps, or accompanied the boys to church. Damaged, she said. He remembers it plainly: damaged, damned, a worn-out dam lapping at her litter, though the pups are all silent and still. He smells an iron torrent of blood like the ewes lambing in the shed, and Amos scrambles back in revulsion, but there it is, squealing between his hot wet thighs, fur flattened with slick, its long ears pinned back as if straining to make out a threat. Its shrill defiant cry sets Amos wailing in return. He gathers the hare to his heaving chest and presses his slippery fingertips to its eyelids, pleading with them to open, to acknowledge him, to just be careful, fragile thing, to survive this time, to fight the urge to die before life has even begun—

"Time to go, sirrah," coos a voice he doesn't recognise, a woman's, rum dark and irresistible. He looks around, but he can't see another soul in the windswept field, not so much as a rook.

He turns back to the hare and smooths the rumpled fur of its brow with the stump of his ring finger. Black stitches pucker the skin, a perfect match for the creature's whiskers.

"Come," the woman tells him. "Feast."

On my insistence, we took a light supper of cold chicken and weak ale before heading out to terrorise the highway. Edward was fidgeting with excitement. He kicked me beneath the table.

"This sheep farm of yours," he said, "what would I do there?"

I looked up, trying to keep the eagerness from my eyes. He had never brought the subject up before. I shrugged; he would lose interest if I looked desperate. "Frighten off wolves," I said, and stuffed my mouth to keep from saying more.

"There's no wolves left in England," he said glumly. "Not since the old Queen died."

I paused with a strip of chicken skin at my lips. "Queen Anne died? When?"

"I don't know. Years ago. We've got a German king now. Does news not reach Suffolk?"

I scratched at my scalp. I worried about my brain sometimes. Too much sun, perhaps, sitting out by the millpond on my own. But I felt that summer optimism now, watching Edward meander towards safety, boring and ordinary, and ours. I would buy a flock at auction, and he would fix us up a neat little paddock. Perhaps my father's dull instructions would be mesmerising in my hands, showing Edward the conjurer's trick of wool, how to turn raw fleece into something bright and covetable.

"Do you think—"

He waved a chicken bone, slick with grease. "One more coach, then we move on. And you'll come, Aim, won't you? To Cornwall or Norfolk or whatever little tedious backwater—"

"Yes," I said. I could do nothing else.

It was not our last robbery, nor even the second-to-last.

I once believed my life had no purpose or direction. That nothing I did or said was of any consequence. I was a flimsy thing buffeted by winds I neither perceived nor understood. But in Edward's presence, I felt like every minute decision of mine was heavy with cosmic consequence. If I failed to amuse Edward at breakfast, he might seek out a brawl by noon. If I glanced too long at a farrier's shop, Edward would catch a mania for horse theft. That would become our life for a month or two, until his whim was quenched. If I was remiss and didn't lock away our earnings in time, Edward would lose them at cards. If I counted them carefully and put them out of his reach, he would take to his bed in a funk that was mine to fix. I cleaned his wounds and watched the highways for danger; I nursed his sore head when he'd been in his cups; I kept his coat buttoned against the wind as if he were a child, even when the buttons were flaked with the blood of the fools who stood between Edward and his wants. Love fastened me to him like shackles of lead.

It couldn't save him.

They sent a runny-nosed reverend down to the cells to comfort us in our last days. I lay in the corner on some straw, leaving the bed for Edward. The reverend sat with him, noisily clearing his sinuses every minute or so. Marvellous: Edward and I would go to the gallows with a raging cold.

"I will pray with you," said the reverend, "if you'll allow it."

Edward shook his head, eyes drifting to the slit of window up near the ceiling. We could hear the carriages in the street outside, the cries of the costermongers and the link boys cursing as they dodged mounds of dung. "Can never tell who's listening," he said.

We would die together. All at once it became real to me: the reverend's black vestments, the cobwebs draping the cell's vaulted ceiling, the piss pot we'd been left to share. My parents would hear of this. Perhaps they would see my likeness in some broadsheet and feel a tingle of recognition. I could not recall their faces now, nor even their names – perhaps they had forgotten me too. A sob escaped me, and Edward heard it. I expected to see resentment in his eyes, but he turned his face to the reverend and spoke softly.

"The rumours that I killed a recruiter in Bristol: they're true. And before that, there was a stranger in London, Wapping way – I took his purse and dabbed him when he struggled. Don't know who he was, but his death is on me. A year or two prior, I fled the Navy the moment we made port. They'd flogged all the obedience out of me; this is what's left. Might as well hang me for all of it."

I knew none of this. My mouth dried up as I considered how to comfort him. "You were surviving…" I began, but he waved me silent.

"I could have survived on a tedious little sheep farm. I just didn't fancy it." He rubbed at his face. We had no washing facilities, and the cell's dirt had crept all over him, dulling his skin like a treasure hidden in the muck of the street. He sighed. "I've been alone my whole life. Even when I was small, I fought like a cat when my mother tried to hold me—"

I wanted to speak, to reassure him, but the reverend cut in with a verse:

"When I was a child, I spoke as a child, I understood as a child, I thought as a child: but when I became a man, I put away childish things."

Edward held out his hand, showed the reverend the ring on his slender finger, the golden skull cheerful as ever. "I found it in the mud on the foreshore after I killed that stranger. I meant to wash off the blood, perhaps drown myself – I don't know. But I read the name engraved inside and… well, I was fanciful. As a boy, did you ever dream up a playmate?"

This, too, I did not know. Some rare part of Edward kept hidden from me.

He sucked in a breath. "I ran away to sea at ten. A moment's impulse I'd regret all my life. When I finally took the chance to desert, I journeyed home only to find a new family occupied our house. Mother had died long ago. They'd even turned her cats out onto the street." He wet his cracked lips. "She promised me she'd always protect me and watch over me, but she couldn't, not in the end, not when I finally wanted it. I hated her for being so unlike other mothers. No respectable woman talks to spirits in the mirror. They don't sell acorns to ward away lightning strikes."

He paused, having exhausted himself with the truth. The reverend wisely kept silent.

"More than that," Edward went on, "I hated myself for running away, for needing excitement. And the guilt only made the impulse worse. The thieving and the gambling and the fighting, it kept me alive. And Aim—"

The reverend nodded. "They told me you speak of an accomplice."

He gave a wan smile. "My accomplice."

"Edward—" I started, but he ignored me.

He twisted off the ring with difficulty. I'd never seen him without it; a vertiginous feeling, like watching him walk away without a backward glance. He turned it in his fingers for a moment before handing it to the reverend. "Take it. Sell it, maybe. Alms for the poor, to weigh against my soul."

The reverend did so with a great sniff, and held it up to the window to better examine the engraving inside.

"Aimee Hynde, obt 1713 Æt 19," he said. "Someone's tragedy, almost twenty years past."

The street outside was quiet. The costermongers and the carriages had paused their racket, stopped dead like my breath.

Edward rubbed at the groove on his ring finger. "Someone's tragedy. But for a while, my friend."

My heart *thumpa-thumpa*'d in my ears. I scrambled to my feet, sending straw flying. "Edw—"

The hangman's trap swung open beneath me, sending me plummeting into a dark, forgetful chamber.

I am in my bed, swaddled in woollen blankets. The fever has passed. I look down at the ball of bandages that is my hand and wonder at it. I can feel my whole finger still, though I know it is the physician's possession now, taken with him to be burned or displayed in a jar of alcohol. I kick off my sweaty bedspreads and shuffle to the edge of the bed, setting my feet down on the cool floorboards, heavenly after my ordeal. No one is watching me through the night. They must all be abed, I tell myself, and gingerly stand to see if they have left me a pitcher of water. After the fever, I am parched.

I turn too fast, almost succumbing to dizziness. The room is small all of a sudden, or perhaps I am tall now, long-legged and strong like my brothers. The smell of cooking and washing and rank close quarters living threatens to turn my stomach. A string of drying clothes bisects the room: women's things, much mended and brown with age. I do not know this place, its mean sooty windows, nor its tallow candles trailing black threads of smoke.

To my surprise, there's a woman on the bed, hunched over a kitchen pan. She's whispering to herself, strange words in a foreign tongue, and I smell the Popery on her as strong as the mould spreading over the walls. In her fist is a ribbon of crinkled black hair. She lays it in the pan with care. I hear a rattling beneath the bed, a struggling bundle of claws, and before I can open my dry mouth to confront the woman, she reaches down and drags a dark something out into the candlelight, bound in twine like a cut of beef. A knife follows, and I hear a high whine escape from my own lips as I realise what I am about to witness.

The woman passes the blade through the hare's throat, soothing it through its death throes, and guides the fount of blood into the pan as best she can. Filigree words roll off her tongue. I recognise the names of the apostles jumbled in with nonsense such as a drunk might mutter at the moon. She is a handsome woman, not some malevolent crone. I see cats in the room's dark corners, six of them, watching me with shining eyes.

"Go to him," she says, when the pan is almost full.

"What is this?" I choke.

She cannot hear me. "Tend to him."

"Who are you?"

With a gasp, she looks up. She stares at me, wide-eyed, not mad but full of sober intent. I am an intruder in her lonely little home, but she views me not with surprise, but gratification.

In the pan of blood and hair, I see my face. Lips blue as frost on a millpond. And my eyes: moon-cracked amber.

"Edward," she chants, her gaze meeting mine. "Edward."

I know no one by that name.

Her eyes brim with tears. The house is empty, I realise. Just this woman and her cats and the girls who come to her for pennyroyal tea. The churchyard holds her husband and her babies, and now she fears the sea may take the only thing she has left.

She holds the pan aloft, bids me drink. My mouth aches for moisture and I drink with gratitude. It is, I dimly recall someone telling me, a gesture of comradeship.

|Acknowledgements|

This collection of weird preoccupations wouldn't exist without the support of so many people. These are a few, but by no means all:

Betty, much missed, who I know is cheering me on from her starlit garden. We are footsoldiers in the war against despair.

David Southwell, creator of Hookland, for all his generosity over the years. I hope you enjoy what I've done with the ghost soil.

Dad, for always answering my extremely specific Naval history questions.

Steve at Black Shuck Books, for making this collection happen.

Bernie, who is probably still standing at that bus stop.

And, as always, big beams of gratitiude go to my Patreon supporters for their friendship and kindness. It really does mean the world.

Verity Holloway lives in East Anglia. She is the author of novels *The Others of Edenwell*, *Pseudotooth*, and *Beauty Secrets of the Martyrs*, the graphic novel *Gore*, and *The Mighty Healer*, a biography of her quack doctor ancestor. She writes folklore features for *Hellebore Zine* and her short fiction has appeared in British Fantasy Society *Horizons*, *The Flame Tree Book of Horror* series, and *The Ghastling*, among others. Find her at verityholloway.com and on Twitter as @verity_holloway.